PIRU LOVE

Kre Kre

To Nabou
Appreciate the
Purchase Her
Much Love Fro
Athens to Mazz
Damu Love

Please join us on the following Social Networks:
www.kalikrepublications.com
www.facebook.com/kalikrepublications
kalikre@gmail.com
Blog: http://kalikre.wordpress.com/

PIRU (pīe-roo) n. 1. A Blood Gang originated in Compton, California, in the early 70's. 2. A street that starts in Los Angeles, East of San Pedro Street and ends at South Mona Blvd in Compton. 3. A person who identifies themselves as an affiliate of a group that wears burgundy, or red attire.

LOVE (luv) n. 1. A deep and tender feeling of affection for attachment or devotion to a person or persons. 2. A feeling of brotherhood and good will toward other people. 3. Strong liking for or interest in something.

July 10, 1987   Friday 11:45 a.m.

ONE

"Solomon! Solomon!" yelled Chinadoll, walking into the living room from the kitchen, dressed in tight red sweat pants, a K.C. Chiefs football jersey and a red bandana tied onto her head, aunt jemima style, holding a pack of Newports in her hand.

"Yes, momma" Solomon responded, breathing heavily from the sprint from his bedroom. Seconds later, his two brothers Maurice and Kyle arrive to be nosy.

"Have you been in my fucking Newports blood?" She asked through a set of clenched teeth.

Solomon's feelings were crushed from the question, because they both know he doesn't smoke. Today is his seventeenth birthday and he's long overdue for some affection from his mother. His eyes widen from fear, while forming a lump in his throat. He pretty much knew where she was going with that question, so he prepared by balling up both fists. "No momma, I didn't touch your cigarettes, I don't smoke," he responded, locking eyes with her.

"You little lying muthafucka! You ain't shit! You just like your daddy, you cracker muthafucka!" Chinadoll yelled, from the top of her voice with her finger pointed in his face. She couldn't stand Solomon. Their relationship has been this way since he was brought into this world, realizing that Solomon wasn't a product of her husband. Chinadog used to pimp her out to a white trick who paid well. This went on twice a week for months, even

1

several months into her pregnancy. Once Chinadog took one look at Solomon during birth, he felt betrayed and divorced Chinadoll. She was scorned. Deep down inside she knew she was wrong for taking it out on Solomon, but could care less. "Maurice, get on that nigga blood!"

On command, Maurice struck Solomon with a fury of blows, landing most of them on top of his head and face, dropping him onto the floor.

With the swiftness, Solomon bounced back onto his feet exchanging blows with Maurice. This went on for fifteen seconds with Solomon getting the best of him. Maurice stumbled backwards into the china cabinet, bumping his head; he was out cold. Solomon bounced in place throwing several jabs into the air, like a professional boxer.

"Reese! Reese! Get yo' ass up blood!" China yelled, shoving a cigarette into her mouth and lighting it. She was highly disappointed at Maurice. This is Chinadog's son by another woman. However, the two raised him ever since he was nine months old, when they first met. Chinadoll is the only mother that he knows. His birth mother is somewhere in the City of Compton, smoked out on P.C.P. Chinadoll looked over at Kyle, who was waiting nervously. "Get that fool blood!" China demanded.

Kyle nervously rushed at Solomon trying to tackle him. Solomon stepped into a left jab, striking him in the face, then followed up with a short right hook to the jaw, knocking him to the ground, landing inches from Chinadog's shrine; which consisted of a dresser stand full of gang photos, red bandanas, a

2

throwback Pittsburg Pirates baseball cap, a pair of Stacy Adams and a walking cane. If Kyle would've knocked the shrine down, he would've been in trouble. China becomes more upset as she watches Kyle pull a stunt, like he's dazed.

"Get your punk ass up blood and stop faking. Both of y'all!" China ordered, as the two slowly rose to their feet, shaking off the dizziness. She walked over to the ashtray that was on the glass table and took one last drag before disposing the cigarette. She looked over at Solomon with malice in her eyes. "You think you tough huh? You little zebra looking muthafucka. You ain't did nothing blood. You ain't did shit!"

Tears formed in the wells of Solomon's eyes as he exited the living room, heading out the front door.

Kyle walked up to China holding his jaw. "Momma-"

"Shut your soft ass up! Both of you niggas are busters, get out of my face!" China shouted, who was irritated by their actions.

Maurice and Kyle walked off holding their heads in shame.

China fired up another Newport, while walking over to her stereo system. She twisted a few knobs until the intro of her favorite song came on. She began dancing while flashing gang signs in the form of a "P" to the song "Rockberry," by the L.A. Dream Team.

Solomon stopped in the front yard for a moment, drying his eyes, trying to gain his composure. He exhaled as he wiped his forehead clear of the sweat that formed from the eighty-degree weather and the scuffle that took place inside. The heat caused him to remove his t-shirt, tossing it onto the hood of China's white 1976 Chevy, that's parked in the driveway. He adjusted his charcoal gray khaki pants, while tucking his tank top t-shirt inside of them.

"Happy Birthday brother!" Deena and Sabrina sung in unison from across the street. The twins love Solomon dearly.

Solomon becomes excited by hopping the fence with one hand, dashing across the street to his grandmother's front yard where the twins are standing. He ran up on the two giving them hugs and kisses. They kissed him in return, Solomon blushed profusely. He had a wonderful but strange relationship with his sisters.

"Thank you", Solomon replied, as he pulled back from the two.

"Why is the side of your face red?" asked Deena, the oldest twin, who also treats him more like her favorite son.

Solomon hesitated before answering. "Momma asked me did I smoke her cigarettes. When I told her no, she made Maurice and Kyle jump me. After I beat them both up, she got mad."

Deena becomes furious. "What?! On your birthday?!"

Solomon nodded in agreement.

Deena looked across the street towards her mother's home and to no surprise; China was standing in the doorway, nodding her head to the music, with a Newport in between her lips. Deena marched in her direction.

4

Deena and Sabrina who are nineteen years old, are the oldest of China's four children. Second is Kyle, who is eighteen, then Solomon who is seventeen years of age. All the siblings are a mixture of African American and Cambodian; except for Solomon who is black, Cambodian and white. Even though Maurice is their half-brother, they didn't care too much for him. He's twenty years old.

The twins felt Maurice envied Solomon because of his looks. Genetically, you can see the different trait in each child. The twins look exactly like Chinadoll when she was their age; caramel brown, with coal black hair, petite coke bottle figures and their signature small pea shape heads with slanted devilish looking light brown eyes. Kyle looked exactly like his sisters, but with a more masculine touch and wore his hair in a short curly style. Maurice didn't have any special features about himself. He is five feet nine, one hundred and sixty pounds, oily black complexion, with short nappy hair and yellow teeth that are stacked on top of each other. He took his mother's side of the family.

Solomon, who gets all the attention out of the group, stands at five feet nine, one hundred and fifty-two pounds of chiseled lean beef. His butter yellow complexion, complimented his coal black shoulder length hair that he always wore in French braids. What drove the young girls wild, was his emerald green eyes and European shaped nose. However, he had the same facial features as his sisters, brother and mother.

Sabrina pulled Solomon by the arm. She knew her sister was about to chastise their mother and didn't want him to see it. "Come on, granny wanna wish you a happy birthday."

Chinadoll thumped the remainder of the cigarette into the grass, as Deena entered the yard through the front gate. "It's a beautiful day, don't you think?" China asked, closing her eyes inhaling the fresh air, trying to be funny. "Look, miss me with that! You know today is your son's birthday. Why you have him fighting his brothers?" Deena asked, walking up on her mother.

"Because someone was in my damn cigarettes!" China shot back, getting into her daughter's face.

"Back up," Deena said, placing her hands-on China's chest, pushing her back softly. "So, you automatically assumed it was Solomon?"

"Of course, that little low life muthafucka can't be trusted. He's just like his daddy, fucking white devil. I can't stand that little dirt bag. He's the reason why your father left me, shit." China explained, trying to make sense of her foolishness.

Deena looked at her mother, shaking her head in disbelief. "Are you serious?"

"On Piru Blood," China shot back, flashing a Piru sign with her right hand, showing her seriousness.

"He had no control over your actions. That was your choice. I wish you would grow up and be a mother to your child, before he looks for it elsewhere," Deena explained.

"Shit, I am a mother to him. You see he has a place to lay his fucking head at night," China responded, rolling her neck. "Not only that, I'm doing this shit all by myself. I don't have a clue as to where his father is, cracker muthafucka!"

"Well, you made that choice, so deal with it." said Deena. "Why don't you at least give your son a hug and tell him happy birthday. I'm willing to bet that will make his day."

Chinadoll pondered on that thought, becoming happy. "I know, I plan on baking him a cake later on today. That's my baby," China replied sarcastically, with a devilish smirk on her face.

Being bipolar was unheard of in the eighties, especially amongst African Americans. But Chinadoll was most definitely a bipolar case. She hasn't seen a doctor since Solomon was born, so it hasn't been revealed to her yet.

Deena smacked her teeth. "You've been saying that every year, for the past ten years. Alright, I'm telling you now, it's gonna come back and bite you on the ass. Watch what I tell you, karma's a bitch." Deena explained, pointing her finger at China, as she exits the yard through the front gate.

"Get outta my yard, heifer! Since y'all love him so much, how come he doesn't live over there with y'all, huh?! Why don't you, your sister and grandmother take care of him?!" China shouted, slowly walking to the yards front gate.

"Shut up and go in the house!" Deena shouted in reply, as she sashayed across the street in a white long sleeve button down

7

guess shirt, with matching tight fitting guess jeans and a pair of red sandals.

"That's what I thought!" China shot back, instantly becoming furious. She walked in the middle of a hundred and twenty ninth street, venting out to anybody who wanted to listen. This is a routine that happens every two or three weeks. From China's actions, one would think that she abuses drugs. However, her drug is a pack of Newports and a can of Olde English 800 beer, that she consumes on a daily basis.

Deena turns around and shakes her head at her mother, out of disgust. "You're thirty-five and a mess."

Sabrina, Solomon and their grandmother walks out to the front yard and watch, as China makes a fool of herself.

"Linda! Linda! Go in the house!" yelled Ms. Spencer, a petite framed, fifty-five-year-old Cambodian woman, with salt and pepper hair pulled into a coif, wearing Malcolm-X stylish glasses, dressed in a red robe and matching corduroy house shoes. This is Chinadoll's mother. She walked into the middle of the street, to console her daughter, who was down on her knees crying profusely, talking to herself. She walked her daughter back into her yard, while her grandchildren looked on. Ms. Spencer understood her daughter's adversities firsthand. Their history is similar.

In 1950; twenty-one-year-old Calvin and eighteen-year-old Susan Spencer were pronounced husband and wife. Calvin was a tall dark and handsome black man, serving in the army, stationed somewhere in Cambodia. He met Susan and ninety days later, they were married. The happy couple moved to Los Angeles in 1951 and Susan gave birth to her first child, a boy name Walter. A year later Linda was born.

The Spencer's were the only bi-racial family on a hundred and twenty ninth street. This neighborhood at one time was totally white. African Americans did not invade the city of Compton, until the early sixties.

In 1965, Calvin was sent to Vietnam to fight in the war. A month later he was killed, leaving Susan to raise two children on her own. Ten months later Susan landed a job to support her family, then out of nowhere fifteen-year-old Walter gets hit by a drunk driver and dies right in front of their home.

Susan remained strong and continued to raise Linda the best way she could. She never remarried, but had a live-in boyfriend to bring a family balance inside her household. Her boyfriend was a 35-year-old black man, who sexually and verbally abused Linda while Susan was out earning a living. This caused Linda to act out by talking back to her mother and running away from home occasionally.

A year later, fifteen-year-old Linda met eighteen-year-old Chinadog, and his toddler son Maurice. The following year, Linda became pregnant with twins and two years later, her and Chinadog were married and moved into the house across the street   from   her   mother.

July 4, 1984   Sunday 9:30 p.m.

TWO

THREE YEARS AGO

Crack cocaine was born and the influx was phenomenal. In this area P.C.P. is the drug of choice and Chinadog was a notorious sherm head.

The intersection of Avalon and El Segundo Boulevard is congested with stop and go traffic, due to Chinadog directing cars in the nude, under the influence of P.C.P., with all red high top Chuck Taylors on. This is common for thirty-five-year-old Chinadog, a reputable and original member of the West Side Piru Blood gang. Fifteen minutes later, two patrol cars from the Carson Sheriff pulls into the intersection, to peacefully remove Chinadog.

"Hey, Chinadog, get out of the freaking street!" yelled an officer, over the car's loud speaker. This is Officer Buttox, a white man in his mid-thirties, who's been knowing Chinadog for three years now. "Chinadog, you have to get out of the street. Tax paying citizens are trying to return home from work and you're making it hard to do so."

After five minutes of trying to smooth talk Chinadog, the cops decided to take action. Officer Buttox and his partner Henderson parks the vehicle alongside the curb and exits.

"Come on Chinadog, let's get out of the street so people can return home," said Buttox, grabbing China; slowly walking him to the sidewalk, in front of a Burger King restaurant.

Two more sheriff deputies approach Chinadog, with flashlights in hand. This is Officer Esson, a thirty-five-year-old

10

white male, who has been on the force for ten years. Officer Milano, is a thirty-two-year-old Italian male who has been a sheriff for five years and already has a reputation for being an asshole. He also knows Chinadog well.

On each corner of the intersection of El Segundo and Avalon are shopping centers. This is where eighty percent of the traffic is coming from. Shopping patrons, residents of the neighborhood and Piru members, watch closely, from every corner as the police deals with Chinadog.

"Well, well, well, look what we have here," said officer Milano, being sarcastic, shining the light in Chinadog's face, looking into his pupils. "Oh, yeah, just like I figured, he's high off that water, that sherm, better known as butt naked."

Officer Esson flashes his light onto China's nine inch dangling flaccid penis. "Jesus Christ, look at the hose on that fucker."

"Stop doing all that gay shit, blood!" shouted a Piru member from across the street. It's obvious that the officers were fascinated with his manhood.

Officer Milano removes the light from China's face and points the light into the crowd of onlookers across the street. "Clear the sidewalk people let's go!"

"We ain't going nowhere blood, this our hood fool!" yelled a Piru member.

Officer Milano took the light off the crowd and placed his flashlight back into the ring on his belt. "Alright Chinadog, you're going to jail buddy for indecent exposure, come on."

Officer Esson finally removed the light from his cock and pointed it towards the ground. Out of nowhere, just as Officer Milano tugged on Chinadog's twenty-two inch biceps, he got a burst of energy.

"AAAAAarrrggghhh!" yelled Chinadog snatching away from Officer Milano, bolting east on El Segundo Boulevard. All three cops became horrified, as Milano's body slung into the brick wall in Burger King's parking lot.

"Don't just stand there, apprehend that son-of-a-bitch!" Milano shouted, staggering back onto his feet, trailing in Chinadog's direction. The other officers followed.

Passing vehicles honked their horns at Chinadog out of love and respect. "Go Chinadog Go!"

Chinadog ran like a slave seeking freedom. Physically, the cops are no match to the two hundred and twenty-pound mass muscle machine, that's a towering, six foot-four and cut up like God chiseled him personally. In the nude, his body resembles the suit on Batman in the movies; black and ripped the fuck up. Plus, being under the influence of P.C.P. doubled his strength, the officers are aware of this, that's why they hesitated when he snatched away from them running.

Officer Milano snatched his walkie talkie from his belt and called for more assistance. "This is Officer 1432, I need assistance. I have a runner under the influence of P.C.P, headed towards Central Avenue," said an exhausted Milano, fighting for air. "Stop you motherfucker!"

Chinadog passed McKinley Street. Moments later, as he approaches Stanford Avenue, two cops are running into his direction; one armed with mace and the other with a night stick. Chinadog showed no signs of stopping, so the officer with the nightstick, tackled Chinadog by the waist. Chinadog drug the officer for several feet, like Christian Okoye used to do in his prime. The other officer sprayed Chinadog in the face. Chinadog screamed like a wild animal, as he rushed the cop. Seconds later, the other four cops arrive to the scene. Officer Milano jumps right onto Chinadog's back and began pounding his head rapidly, with the bottom part of his right fist. The other cops hesitate with sticks in hand, as they watch Milano ride Chinadog's back, like a bucking bull coming out the gate. When the opportunity came, the five officers assaulted Chinadog with their night sticks. They beat Chinadog down something terrible. After he was subdued, they slapped the cuffs on, then occasionally kicked him in the ribs and nuts for giving them a hard time. They stood around Chinadog like a captured animal from the wilderness, laughing and cracking jokes.

"China! China!" Chinadoll yelled, crying hysterically. She tried to break through the cop's circle, to get to her baby daddy, but Officer Buttox grabbed her.

"I'mma go and grab the patrol car," said Esson, to his partner Milano.

"10-4," Milano replied.

"And may I ask, who are you?" asked Officer Buttox.

"Oh, that's his other half, Chinadoll," Milano replied being sarcastic.

"Now, you have a Chinadog and a Chinadoll," Officer Henderson butted in, being an ass-hole. They all double over in laughter. "Now, she looks more like a chink than he does, this son-of-a-bitch is blacker than an ace of spades. Shit, he's blacker than Texas Gold. He looks more like a wet seal than anything."

Truth is, Chinadog was not mixed with any Asian ancestry. He is 100% African American. Chinadog earned his name in elementary school when he was fighting another reputable Piru member by the name of Pudding.

Chinadog, who was getting the brakes beat off of him, kneed Pudding in the solar plexus, knocking the wind out of him, causing him to bend over gasping for air. Chinadog then jumped into the air yelling like Bruce Lee, striking Pudding in the center of the back with an elbow, dropping him face first onto the pavement. From that day on, he was dubbed Chinadog and everyone that witnessed the fight was scared shitless of him

"Officer, can I talk to my baby daddy please?" Chinadoll asked Officer Henderson crying profusely. Henderson looked at Milano, who nodded in approval.

Once he gave the okay, Chinadoll snatched from Henderson and dove on top of the father of her children, crying hysterically. The cops looked on with smirks on their faces.

The cops looked on as she cried on top of him, for three minutes straight.

Officer Henderson tried pulling her away, but she snatched away from him. After a minute or so she sprang onto her feet pissed.

"How come my baby daddy is all beat up blood?" Chinadoll asked firmly, through a set of clenched teeth.

"Well, for starters, he was directing traffic asshole naked in the intersection down the street. That's indecent exposure. And to make matters worse, he assaulted six officers who tried to help him. Need I say more?" explained Officer Milano.

Chinadoll exhaled gaining her composure. Her hatred for the police ran neck to neck, to the hate she had for the Crips, which was deep. "Well, what's gonna happen to him?"

"Well, we're gonna take him down to Killer King and get him some medical attention first," Milano explained, rocking from heel to toe.

Martin Luther King Jr. Hospital, is located in Compton and earned its name Killer King; for the many people who check in for minor problems and leave out in a coroner's van. However, they have the number one trauma center in the nation for gunshot victims.

Esson pulls up in the patrol car. Officer Milano and Buttox places Chinadog into the backseat.

"After we take him to the hospital, he's going to jail for indecent exposure. We'll let him sit in the drunk tank until he sobers up. You can bring him some clothes, he'll get cited out at the station," officer Milano explained, as he climbed into the driver's seat, while Esson flopped into the passenger's side.

Chinadoll exhaled as she gave Milano the evil eye. Both officers slammed their doors and sped off into traffic, heading east on El Segundo Boulevard in the direction of the hospital. The other four cops left the scene, leaving Chinadoll alone on the sidewalk, to watch the brake lights on their vehicle vanish into thin air. Chinadoll grew an eerie feeling.

*****

One hundred and thirty second street in-between Wilmington Boulevard and Grandee Avenue, is heavily populated with residents from the neighborhood; mostly Compton Crips. This area is known as Original Front Hood. Members from this gang are rivals to all Pirus and will kill one on sight, if they catch one slipping. Sudden outburst of M-80's go off every other minute, causing Officer Milano and Officer Esson to jump or look over their shoulders, making sure those are fireworks and not gunfire. The patrol car pulls to the middle of the block, in front of a group of Crips standing on the curb and around a 79' Monte Carlo on lace rims.

"Hey, was'sup cuz?" asked Milano, as he rolled down the window.

"Aw, ain't shit cuz, cripping as usual," Neckbone responded, flashing a Crip sign with his right hand. Neckbone walks up to the car. "Who you got in the backseat cuz? One of the homies?"

Both officers chuckle. "Nawh, we got one of your favorites back there. That's O.G. Chinadog from West Side Piru," Milano explained, smiling.

"What?!" Neckbone flashed, losing his cool. He's heard of Chinadog, but never seen him in person. He snatched a blue rag from his left back pocket and waved it up and down into the air with force, hoo-banging on Chinadog.

Several Crips joined in on the free recreation. "Fuck Piru cuz, this Compton Crip!" Chinadog sat up in the back seat with gashes on his head and blood streaming down the side of his face, still under the influence. He has no clue as to where he's at. A year ago, Chinadog was picked up for the murder of Casper, one of Neckbone's homeboy who was a reputable Crip and loved dearly by other Crips throughout Compton. He beat the case due to lack of evidence and technicalities within the witnesses.

"Calm down Neckbone, he can't hear you. He's high off that water, that he got over there in Fruit Town. But guess what? We're gonna drop him off around the corner and see if he can find his way back to his hood," Milano explained, with a smirk on his face, winking his eye at the Crips.

Neckbone and his homies backed up to the curb, snickering. "Right on," Neckbone replied. The patrol car sped off, pulling over two blocks away letting Chinadog out the vehicle, then disappeared into thin air.

Chinadog stood on the sidewalk listening to what appears to be fireworks, but sounds more like rounds being fired from a gun. His high goes down a notch. He's starting to feel the pain from the knots that formed on both sides of his head. He touches them as he slowly walks down the sidewalk, unaware of his location.

Out of nowhere, two Crips sprang from in-between two parked cars, jogging towards Chinadog, armed with pistols cutting him off in his path.

One Crip fired two rounds into his chest and one into his stomach. Unfazed by the injuries, Chinadog charged the two Crips. They both back peddled several steps out of fear. The other Crip shot China in the throat twice with a .357 Python; this stopped him in his tracks. He staggered a few steps, then collapsed face first onto the pavement. Chinadog tried to get up, but the two quickly stood over him and emptied their revolvers into his upper back, neck and head, leaving his skull cracked in half with blood and brain matter all over the pavement. His last thought was embedded onto the sidewalk. The Crips fled the scene, vanishing into the noisy Fourth of July atmosphere of fireworks. Their gang status amongst their comrades increased two-folds, for this murder. This was the beginning of one of the most bloodiest and deadliest gang wars, in Compton California.

September 10, 1987   Thursday 2:30 p.m.

THREE

It's another normal day in Compton California. The weather is warm, somewhere in the mid or high seventies. Students at Centennial High School drug their feet in the hallway, as they contemplate ditching their last period class.

Solomon had other plans. He strolled into history class dressed in an all-black khaki suit, with a burgundy Phillies baseball cap and matching burgundy, high top Chuck Taylor tennis shoes on. He removed his cap, revealing his shoulder length hair, that was freshly twisted into French braids. He noticed Tina-ru and flopped down in the desk in front of her. She seductively stroked one of his braids through its entirety.

"Um, Ms. Lucas, that's not appropriate now. Class is over in forty-five minutes, you can fondle his hair after the bell rings," interrupted Mrs. Milano, a thirty-one-year-old Italian school teacher from the city of Carson.

This is her second year at Centennial, she transferred here from Pacific Palisades High School. Mrs. Milano opened the attendance book and took roll.

Tina-ru reached up to Solomon's ear whispering. "Oh, this white chick likes you."

Solomon shook his head in disagreement.

The classroom was half filled with students. After roll was called, Mrs. Milano walked over to both doors of the classroom and secured them.

19

"Okay, everyone, I know this is our third day of class, but yesterday I told you guys to do some homework," Mrs. Milano expressed, as she sat back at her desk. "I want each of you to stand before the class and tell me how your summer went and what activities you participated in." All the students nervously looked around at each other, wondering who was gonna have the balls to go first. "Everybody don't go at once. Now if no one goes up, I can randomly pick someone from my attendance sheet," Mrs. Milano explained, folding her arms across her chest exhaling.

"Alright, I'll go first," said Tina-ru, leaping from her chair, sashaying to the front of the class. Tina-ru is average looking, but thick as hell.

Mrs. Milano grew a devilish smirk onto her face. She felt that Tina-ru was wasting her time attending school. This was her second year in her class room. She flunked because she couldn't meet the required credits to graduate. Mrs. Milano felt that sometime this year, Tina-ru would be just another statistic: pregnant, jobless, homeless and on welfare or drugs, like most African American women her age.

Tina-ru stood in front of the classroom swinging from side to side, looking at everything in the classroom, except for the students out of nervousness. After Tina-ru broke the ice by telling her story, every student couldn't wait to tell theirs.

Mrs. Milano became bored from the stories told by each student. She felt that every one of them were goofy, but she listened out of maturity and professionalism.

"And last but not least, Mr. Spencer," announced Mrs. Milano, watching Solomon with a keen eye as he stepped to the front of the classroom.

Tina-ru observed Mrs. Milano eyeing Solomon, with lust in her eyes.

"Well, to be honest, my summer vacation was fair, but it could have been better," Solomon explained, removing one of his French braids from the inside of his khaki shirt, as he and the school teacher made eye contact.

"Explain to me, what could have made your summer great" Mrs. Milano responded, adjusting her Gucci eye wear on her face.

"Well, my birthday is in the summer and the only thing that I received was abusive language from my mother and physical abuse from my two brothers, who jumped me at my mother's command. If my mother would've told me Happy-birthday or that she loved me or any type affection in that matter. I would've had the greatest summer in the world," Solomon explained, looking Mrs. Milano in the eyes. She felt his energy and pain. "So, from the abuse that I received in the household, I acted out by participating in gang activity."

The school bell interrupted the moment of silence that came after the speech Solomon gave. All the students gathered their school materials and exited the classroom. Solomon was the last person to gather his belongings. He slapped on his baseball cap and strolled towards the door, as Tina-ru held it open for him.

"Um, Solomon," Mrs. Milano interrupted, in a soft voice breaking his stride.

Solomon turned towards her desk. "Hey, Was'sup?"

"May I have a word with you for a moment please?" Mrs. Milano asked.

"Yeah, sure," Solomon responded, walking towards her desk.

Mrs. Milano looked at Tina-ru, whose body was halfway in the classroom. "Alone please."

Solomon chuckled, as he turned towards Tina-ru. "Hey, blood, I'mma catch up with you later homie."

Tina-ru smacked her teeth and rolled her eyes at the two, as she stormed away from the door. Solomon sat at the desk in front of her and threw his hands up, in a 'what's up' gesture.

Mrs. Milano rose from her chair and slowly walked to the door, looking out the classroom to make sure that they were alone.

"Is that your girlfriend?"

Solomon shook his head "No."

Mrs. Milano blushed. "Oh, I think she likes you," she replied, as she walked back to her desk, leaning against it.

"Why did you ask that?" Solomon asked, eyeing Mrs. Milano's five-foot six, one-hundred-and-twenty-pound curvaceous frame. Once upon a time Mrs. Milano ran track, her evidence is in her fine toned chiseled calves, thighs, hips and ass that's protruding through her beige Chanel skirt; which compliments her matching pumps, silk shirt, eye wear, bronze skin tone and silky black hair that is wrapped into a bun.

"A woman knows," she responded, clearing her throat, preparing to talk to Solomon on a more serious note. "If it is not a problem with you, I wanted to know more about your relationship with your mother and your gang affiliation. "You don't strike me as a gang member."

Solomon blushed at her ignorance. "I don't mind, if I can ask questions in return."

"Sure, you can ask me anything Solomon. How come you laughed just a second ago?"

"I was laughing at your ignorance. You said I don't strike you as a gang member. Well, I don't know where you're from or live but anybody who's been living in L.A. County since the early seventies, should have some knowledge of the Bloods and Crips."

"Yes, I am aware. Bloods wear red and Crips wear blue", she answered proudly, letting him know that she's not a total square. "Why are you wearing burgundy?"

"It doesn't really mean anything. I wear red all the time. Burgundy is just a secondary color that we wear," Solomon explained.

"So, I take it that you're a blood."

"Yeah, I'm from West Side Piru. My set is called the Rolling 130's," he stated proudly, flashing Piru signs with both hands.

"Earlier you said that your mother is abusive towards you. Is that what made you join a gang?"

"Yeah and no." Solomon replied, as he sat up in his chair, preparing to educate Mrs. Milano. "My mother is a Piru also. My sisters and brothers along with myself, were born into this gang lifestyle. A person would think that if your mother is from the hood also, you would automatically get some love from her; but that's not the case."

"Oh, my goodness, are you serious?" interrupted Mrs. Milano, placing her hands-on top of her thirty-six, D-cup sized bust.

"Oh yeah, my whole family is from the hood. My other siblings' father was a known Piru from the hood also. He was killed three years ago, by some crooked cops who dropped him off in a rival Crip neighborhood and got him killed. As a matter of fact, it happened right down the street on Grandee Avenue and a hundred and thirty-first street".

"The police?! Are you serious?" asked a shocked Mrs. Milano, she couldn't fathom the thought of the police participating in that kind of activity. "Did those dirty cops get arrested and thrown in jail?"

Solomon shook his head. "Nawh, I doubt it. That's some normal shit."

"Normal? Oh my goodness," responded Mrs. Milano, shaking her head in disbelief.

"Ever since I was born, my mother kept her distance from me, leaving my twin sisters to raise me. And the cold thing about it is, they're only two years older than me, so they were basically children trying to raise a child. And we both know how children are, they like to experiment with sex and cigarettes. From the ages of ten to fifteen, both of my sisters molested me off and on. I believe they were going through puberty, at twelve years old. First, they use to make me dry hump them. Then after they got burnt out on that, we went through the oral sex phase. After that, the younger twin stopped molesting me; but the oldest one turned it up a notch. She use to make me climb through the

24

window, while she acted like she was sleep and make me rape her and pull her by the hair," Solomon explained.

Mrs. Milano stood speechless from his testimony and for some odd reason, her panties were soaking wet. "Solomon, oh my goodness you've been through so much. Do you know your biological father?"

"No, that's one of the reasons why my mother hates me. I'm a trick baby. Her husband use to pimp her out to my father, who was a trick for extra money." Solomon explained, with a devilish smirk forming on his face. "So, this is why I run with a gang, to get that love from the homies in the streets that I don't get from my mother at home. I know this may sound strange, but when I'm in the streets with my homeboys or home girls it's therapeutic. The Pirus are my family that respects me. They don't shout, yell or scream at me unless I'm wrong. Don't get me wrong, I love my family, but at any given moment, my mother might make my brothers jump me or she'll accuse me for something that I didn't do. As for my sisters, I try to keep my distance from them, because you never know when that perverted behavior may kick back in. I never liked it, I just dealt with it."

"You're not alone Solomon, we all have secrets." Mrs. Milano replied, looking at her watch. "Oh my, time has flown. Well, Solomon I enjoyed talking to you. I've learned a lot about you today. Do you need a ride home?"

"Nawh I'm good, I have a car ma'am. It's not registered to me, but I'm driving it until further notice," he replied, adjusting his baseball cap on his head as he stood up from his desk. "Well, I'll see you later."

"Mrs. Milano eyed Solomon as he walked towards the door. "Solomon?"

Solomon turned around. "Was'sup?"

"I have one more question. Did your mother or anyone else in your household use drugs?"

"I know it's hard to believe, but no. No drugs whatsoever" Solomon answered sincerely.

"Where do you see yourself in the next five years?" asked a curious Mrs. Milano.

Solomon pondered on her question for a moment before answering. "In the next five years, I'll be twenty-two. I honestly see myself being successful, I'm just going through life adversities at the moment. I believe one day my experiences are gonna motivate someone to be the best that they can be. I have to begin by talking it into existence, Solomon responded, with a sincere smile on his face." And you? Where do you see yourself in the next five years, ma'am?"

"I'm not sure, but I know my life is gonna change drastically. But I feel I'm going to enjoy the change," Mrs. Milano replied sincerely, as she grabbed her jacket and Coach handbag, walking towards the door.

"Let me ask you another question Mrs. Milano."

"Go ahead, Solomon," she demanded standing in front of him. She must brace herself mentally, because she knows how sharp he is.

"Are you happily married?"

Mrs. Milano dropped her head. "Solomon, your question is inappropriate and a little too personal don't you think?"

"So, in other words you're not happy. You have a nice size rock on your finger, he must love you," Solomon hinted.

"Money and material items can't buy love Solomon," Mrs. Milano answered, in a low tone.

"Have you ever heard that saying, similarity causes attraction?"

"Yes, I've heard that before Solomon. Why?"

"You and I have similarities. We look for love from the ones we love, but in return we get our feelings hurt. So, we get love from the things we love to do. For me, it's banging with the Pirus. And for you, it's teaching," Solomon explained, making sense.

Mrs. Milano stared deeply into Solomon's eyes, she couldn't believe she was talking to a teenager. What hit Mrs. Milano the most, was that everything he said was true. She glanced at her watch again. "Yes, your statement is true Solomon. You're saying that to say what?"

Solomon chuckled. "I'mma let you ponder on that thought," he responded as he walked off.

Mrs. Milano stood outside the classroom holding the door in awe of Solomon, as he strolled to the students' parking lot.

*****

Solomon opened the door to a black 1986 Nissan Maxima and climbed into the driver's seat. Inside the car was scorching hot, from sitting out in the parking lot soaking up the rays from the sun. Solomon quickly reached underneath the driver's seat retrieving a ten-inch flat head screwdriver. He stuck it inside the dismantled ignition, and fired up the engine. After placing the screw driver underneath the seat, he fumbled with a few knobs turning on the air conditioner and the car radio on AM stereo, 1580 KDAY. He reached inside the glove compartment and put on a pair of brown gloves and grabbed his Taurus 9mm handgun, placing it in his lap. He put the car in drive smashing out of the parking lot. He gets held up at the entrance by the traffic that's flowing in both directions, on El Segundo Boulevard. He removes his baseball cap and tosses it into the backseat, turning up his favorite song on the radio. 'Make the Music with Your Mouth Biz', by Biz Markie. He gets a break in the traffic and speeds off east on El Segundo.

Once Solomon passes Compton Avenue, he keeps his eyes and ears open. He is now entering the Original Front Hood Compton Crip territory.

Although, Centennial High School is ninety percent Piru populated, the other ten percent are attended by Crips from Carver Park, Eight-ball, Holmes Street, Front Hood, Pocket Hood, Mona Park and 126th Street. However, all the Crips leave after lunch. If they're caught after school, it could be fatal. There are only two other high schools in the City of Compton. Dominguez High which is half Pirus and Crips. Then there is Compton High which is one hundred percent Crip populated.

Solomon reaches Grandee Avenue and makes a right turn. As he cruises down the block, two members from Front Hood Crip, dressed in blue from head to toe, are walking a red nose pit bull on the opposite side of the street, in his direction. This is Baby Bone and Midnight.

They both mad dog the black 86' Maxima, as it cruises in their direction. Once they make contact with Solomon's unfamiliar face, they flash gang signs at him to see if their neighborhoods are compatible. They both stop walking, eyeing the vehicle.

"What's up cuz? What that Front Hood Compton Crip like nigga?!" asked Midnight, walking towards the curb, pulling the chain that's around the neck of his pit bull, who is barking at Solomon also.

Solomon couldn't hear what he was saying, being that the air conditioner, radio and windows were up; but he can read his lips perfectly. To make them bring their guards down, Solomon turned down the radio and air conditioner, then slowed the vehicle down, rolling down the window, while sticking his head out. "Hey, was'sup, cuz? I'm Baby Turtle from Santana block. I'm looking for your homie Hen Dog. I wanna buy a couple zips of weed from him."

"Oh, cuz on a hundred and twenty seventh and Grandee, loc," Baby Bone replied, leaning against a chain linked fence in front of someone's home.

"Hold on let me turn around cuz," Solomon explained, He sped off and busted a C.K. (U-turn) on a hundred and thirty second street. Both Crips waited for Solomon. Baby Bone started playing with the pit bull by slapping his mouth and nose, while Midnight pulls his socks up on both legs through his khaki pants. As Solomon heads in the direction of the Crips, he checks his rear view and door mirrors for the police. Everything was clear so he rolled down the passenger's window and cruised alongside the curb to get a good shot. Before Solomon could make a complete stop, Midnight ran up to the passenger's door window excited. "Hey Baby Turtle, was'sup cuz?"

Knock! Knock! Knock!

Before Midnight realized what was going on, he was hit three times. The first bullet caught him in the right eye socket. The other two caught him in the nose and mouth. The force from the bullets caused his lifeless corpse to fall backwards onto the grass area of the curbside. A horrified Baby Bone cleared the fence that he was standing in front of with one hand. Solomon fired three rounds at him as he dashed through the front yard out of fear. The red nose pit bull barked at Solomon.

Solomon silenced his bark by firing one round into his skull, dropping him right next to Midnight. Solomon rolled up both windows and cruised away from the scene snickering.

September 12, 1987   Saturday 1:35 p.m.

FOUR

Solomon struggled with Maurice's luggage but was successful at putting it inside the trunk of his relatives 77' Sedan de Ville Cadillac. Kyle followed up with another suit case placing it in the trunk also. Solomon slammed the trunk shut and watched as his mother becomes over dramatic hugging and kissing Maurice. Kyle walks over to the two joining them in a group hug.

Maurice is going to live with his grandmother on his mother's side of the family in Compton. His grandmother is becoming ill and would like to become better acquainted with her grandson in her last days. Plus, she needs the extra help around the house.

With Maurice out the picture. Solomon felt that his mother would have no choice but to show him some love now, being that him and Kyle are going to be the only ones in the household.

One down and one to go. Solomon thought to himself. He wasn't a hater but he was yearning for her affection. *I'll give her about a month and she'll come around.*

Maurice pulled away from the two as he exited the yard. He walked up to Solomon and gave him a hug. "Be safe blood and take care of moms for me" he replied, ending their conversation with a blood handshake.

"Don't worry blood I will." Solomon replied. He felt that his hug, handshake and advice was phony but he kept a poker face.

Maurice climbed into the passenger side of the vehicle and sped off down the street. Chinadoll and Kyle walked into the house while Solomon leaned against the chain linked fence in front of his home. The pounding bass from a candy green Suzuki Samurai on cookie cutter rims, turns onto the block coming from Towne Avenue. Solomon recognizes the jeep, but kept his eye on it anyway.

The jeep full of females swerved to the curb where Solomon is standing turning down the loud music. "Solo, was'sup blood?" yelled Tina-ru, from the passenger's window.

Solomon walked to the curbside. "Was'sup blood? What's popping?

Where you been blood? I haven't seen you since Thursday."

"Solo, was'sup blood?" interrupted Kay-Kay, Smurf and Vanity in unison. They are also Piru gang members.

Solomon looked inside the jeep. "Hey, was'sup with y'all blood? How y'all doing?"

"So was'sup blood? You quit school or what? The last time I saw you, you were all up in that teacher's face," said Tina-ru. Her actions are becoming obvious that she wants Solomon to bone her.

Solomon chuckled. "You don't like Mrs. Milano huh?"

"Nah, but I see you do." Tina-ru responded rolling her eyes. "I went to class yesterday and when you didn't show up she had a fit. She really had a fit when I told her you were my dude."

Solomon shook his head. "Aw hell nah, you didn't tell her that, did you?"

"Yep, sure did. Was I wrong?" she inquired, with attitude.

"Dead wrong, but it's all good." Solomon replied smiling. " Where are you guys headed?"

"To the Bompton (Compton) Swap Meet." Tina-ru answered.

"Oh yeah, blood, make sure y'all keep your eyes open. A crab got killed two days ago." Solomon mentioned, winking his eye at the jeep full of female Pirus.

"From where?" asked Tina-ru asked, excitedly.

"Over there by Willowbrook Jr. High School." Solomon responded, adjusting his tan khaki pants legs over his red Chuck Taylor tennis shoes.

"Oh yeah? Fuck that crab ass nigga." Tina-ru responded.

"No doubt." Solomon responded, backing up from the jeep, seeing a 1983 beige Cadillac Coupe de Ville on Dayton's and Vogue tires, turning onto the block with force. He eyes the Cadillac until the occupants inside identifies themselves by flashing blood gang signs out the sunroof. This is Blade and J-Bone from 135th street Piru, also known as the Fives. Solomon acknowledges the two by flashing a Piru sign. The car honks the horn in response as it proceeds down the street.

"Well, let us go Mr. Piru, before we end up in Killer King," said Tina-ru, joking.

"Alright, y'all be cool," said Solomon.

"Byyyeee Solo," All the females inside the jeep responded in a seductive tone. Soon after the jeep smashed off the block.

Moments later two Piru members pull up on a red Schwinn Beach Cruiser bicycle. This is Dirt and Klown, two Piru members from his hood.

Dirt is a twenty-one-year-old, five foot ten, one hundred and ninety-eight pound black male; who is also a Y.A. Baby. This is someone who grew up in California Youth Authority; going in as a child and coming out a man. Dirt was captured when he was thirteen years old and wasn't released until he was twenty-one, which was eight months ago. He did time for killing an O.G. Compton Crip from Carver Park at the Watts Parade. Physically Dirt is hard on the eyes. He is caramel brown with shoulder length hair that's in a perm which is pulled into a ponytail. He has a case of severe acne and a face that resembles a baboon. During his incarceration, all he did was fight Compton Crips, lift weights and eat. Across his back in seven inch letters, is a tattoo that reads 'PIRU', which he loves to show off daily by taking off his shirt. He's dressed in burgundy high top Chuck Taylors, burgundy painter pants that are exposing his burgundy boxer shorts and a white tank top t-shirt.

Klown is a nineteen-year-old six foot one, one hundred and seventy pound Puerto Rican man whose skinny built frame is cut to perfection. Klown is a gangster but he loves to crack jokes and act a fool twenty-four seven. He is also easy on the eyes. He flaunts a flawless caramel skin tone with pearly white straight teeth and hazel eyes that compliment his thick eyebrows. He is dressed in a pair of 501 Levi boot cut jeans, black Romeos polished to perfection and a white t-shirt. His hair is braided in a French braid style.

Territorial wise the Rolling 130's area is small.

From east to west they claim Avalon Boulevard, San Pedro Street and Main Street. From north to south they claim El Segundo Boulevard, 129th St., 130th St., 131st St, 132nd St. and 135th St.

Population wise they're deep. Eighty percent of its members are African American. The remainder twenty percent are a mixture of Mexican, Puerto Rican, El Salvadorian, Native American, Laotian, Chinese, Koreans, Samoans and Filipinos.

"Solo, was'sup blood?" Klown asked as he jumped off the handle bars of the beach cruiser.

"Klown, Dirt, what's up big homies?" Solomon asked, giving both of them dap. "Shit, I was on my way to a hundred and thirty-first to slang a few bags of weed so I could buy those new red Fila's at the swap meet. Other than that, just bickin' back being' bool" (kicking back being cool).

"Hey, a ericket got killed, I think two days ago. I was over there in the four line and One Time came through tripping blood. I'm talking about salty, like a police got killed or something." Klown explained. "So, watch out. The fool that got smoked, his brother is some crab fool that has money and he wants revenge. Then the next day the Fruit Town's caught a crab at the gas station on Rosecrans and Wilmington and blew him out of his truck."

"Yeah, they might creep through here trying to catch the homies slipping." Dirt explained. "Jump on the back of the bike, I'll give you a ride around the corner blood."

Klown jumped back onto the handle bars of the bike while Solomon mounted himself on the set of pig nuts that's screwed onto the back rim of the bike. Dirt zig zagged a few feet before he picked up enough speed to gain control of the bike. The ride from 129th street to 131st was a breeze. As they rode several feet into the block, Solomon jumped off the pig nuts and walked up to his homeboy Nueve, which means nine in Spanish, who is sitting in a red wheelchair in front of his house with a nine millimeter underneath his seating cushion.

Nine is a twenty-five-year-old, Mexican American man and a high ranking Piru gang member. He earned his name because of the multiple times he's been shot. Nine has survived two comas, both due to gang related shootings. He's been stabbed in the state prison system by Surenos because of his affiliation with the Pirus. He was also acquitted on two separate murder charges. The first one was against Javier Pena, a Mexican dealer who was killed for three kilos of powder. The second one was against a Compton Crip from Mona Park whose riddled body was lumped over the steering wheel of an El Camino truck at the light on 135th and Avalon Boulevard.

"Nine, was'sup big homie?" asked Solomon, giving him a pound.

"Shit, I'm trying to be like you lil homie." Nine responded with a smile on his face.

"Be like me? Shit, I'm trying to be like you big homie." He responded pulling his Rolex band necklace inches from his chest, then letting it go.

"This ain't nothing but material items homie." Nine explained. "You're young, by the time you reach my age, you'll have achieved way more than me homie, real talk."

"You think so?" Solomon asked out of curiosity.

"I know so. I compare you to the other homies your age and none of them are as sharp as you. Don't get me wrong, I love the homies to death, but you're a diamond that hasn't been polished yet," explained Nine. "You don't drink or do drugs, stay that way blood."

Solomon pondered on Nine's advice and locked everything he said to him in his memory. "I will blood, on Piru. But in the meantime, how can I shine like you?" Asked Solomon referring to Nine's Rolex necklace, matching bracelet, 24 karat presidential watch and the set of 3 karat F-one round shape diamonds in his left ear.

There wasn't nothing that Nine wouldn't do for his homies. Over the years Nine has made over a quarter of a million dollars by selling twenty dollar bags of high grade weed on this block. So, he wasn't pressed for money. His driveway has a midnight black 1988' Silverado truck on chrome 15x8 Dayton's and a fire engine red 62' Chevy Impala low-rider on 13x8 chrome Dayton rims. Even though his house is equipped with all the amenities, this is just a hangout for the Pirus. He owns a home in Apple Valley.

"Here lil homie." Nine replied, unscrewing the back of one of the diamonds in his ear giving it to him.

Solomon opened his hand, while Nine dropped the gem and the back piece into it. He quickly ran to the driveway using the mirror of the Silverado, to put the earring in his ear. Once the diamond was secured, he slightly rotated his head, watching the diamond dance, as it reflected off the sunlight. Solomon formed a Kool-Aid smile, as he walked back to where Nine is posted. "Thanks, big homie." said Solomon.

"Here blood, take this chain off my neck." demanded Nine.

"Big homie, I'm good blood, this earring is enough," responded Solomon. He was only trying to talk Nine out of one piece of jewelry, not two.

"Blood come get this chain off my neck homie." Nine demanded, becoming serious. He didn't have to ask twice. Solomon removed it from around his neck, like he was robbing Nine.

Solomon felt ten feet tall after securing the chain around his neck. "Hey homie, much love blood." Solomon replied, giving him some dap.

"Oh, you shining now homie," said Nine, admiring the pieces on Solomon. "I still got a few pieces left to shine with. I only wear that shit to catch the bitches."

"When did you get that tat done?" Solomon asked, noticing the prayer hands tattooed on his forearm in red scribe. Above the tattoo reads: "O.G. KHINADOG W.I.P" (West-in-piece).

Nine glances at his forearm. "I got this about a month ago," Nine explained. This is just one of many tattoos Nine has on his body. He has a tattoo of a hand flashing a "P" sign on the back of his bald head. On his neck is the letters C.K. with an X through the C showing his hatred for the Crips. He sports a beige khaki short set with a short sleeve shirt, with a crispy pair of burgundy Nike Cortez and a matching Philadelphia Phillies baseball cap.

"Hey blood, has it been rolling?" Solomon asked, referring to the weed clients.

"Hell nawh, I've been out here for an hour and I ain't sold one bag blood." Nine responded, adjusting his baseball cap. "I don't know what the fuck is going on."

"I got a couple of bags I'm trying to get off dog." Solomon explained, pulling out three dub sacks of chocolate bud.

Nine noticed a van cruising down Towne Avenue as if the occupants inside were observing the block. This is common practice for Crips to sneak by to see how many bloods are hanging out so they can make their move. "Blood that's the third time that van came through here in the last hour. Those are some crabs or the police homie." said Nine, pulling a 9mm from underneath his seat cushion and placing it onto his lap.

"Blood, you got some more heat?" asked a nervous Solomon.

"Yeah, lift up the tarp on the back of the truck." Nine responded.

Solomon went to the back of the truck pulling up the tarp, grabbing the AR-15 rifle and placing it between the Low Rider and the brick wall in Nine's driveway. "If they come through here one more time, I'mma dump on their asses."

Thirty minutes has gone by and the first weed client pulls up to the curbside, which is a carload of women in a brown 83' Fleetwood Brougham. "Can I get two bags of weed?" asked the female passenger.

"Yeah, but you got to get out the car," Nine responded, he was suspicious of these bitches because he has never seen them before.

A five foot six, one-hundred-and-twenty-pound black woman exits the passenger's side of the vehicle, wearing a pair of black stretch pants, with matching shirt and matching open toe sandals. Facial wise she could pass for Tisha Campbell's twin sister. She was high yellow and wore her hair in braids. Body wise, she is thick as hell. Her titties are average, but she has a huge ass. She sashayed towards Nine with a smile on her face. "I wanted to get two dub sacks." the female replied, pulling out forty dollars from her pants pocket.

Nine studied her with a straight face, while digging for a few bags underneath the cushion of his wheel chair. "Here you go." Nine responded, handing her the weed, in return she gave him the money.

Solomon sat on the trunk of Nine's 62' Chevy in the driveway, watching the transaction go down.

"Thank you," the female responded, as she sashayed back to the vehicle.

"You welcome." Nine replied, eyeing the female, trying to remember where he knew her from.

The female gets back into the car and drives off.

"Damn, that bitch was kind of thick huh?" asked Solomon, grabbing his crotch with a smile on his face.

"Yeah, I know that hoe from somewhere blood. I can't put my finger on it right now, but I know her. I think that bitch was a ericket (Crip) blood." Nine explained, smiling.

Thirty minutes later, the jeep full of female Pirus pulls alongside the curb, exiting the vehicle, hyped.

"Blood, we just had a shoot-out with some crab bitches in a brown Brougham." said Tina-ru with a .380 automatic handgun in her hand.

"Homie you were right." Solomon added, walking up to Nine's wheelchair.

"I told you blood! I told you! I don't forget a face homie!!" Nine expressed, becoming loud, shaking his head smiling.

"Y'all knew them crab bitches blood?" Asked Kay-Kay, who is five foot seven, one hundred and thirty pounds of coffee colored curves. She also wears her hair in a braided basket weave hairstyle.

"Let me find out you've been creeping with some crab (Crip) bitches blood." Vanity said to Nine, giving him the evil eye while folding her arms across her thirty-six D-cup bust. Vanity and Nine have a secret sexual relationship. That's how she got the Suzuki Jeep and keeps her five foot six, caramel curvy frame, in all the latest fashion. He also keeps her shoulder length hair done on a weekly basis.

"Nawh, them hoes just left here buying some weed from me." Nine explained, adjusting his baseball cap.

"What?!" asked a furious Tina-ru. "Oh, hell no!"

"Yeah blood on Piru. I think them hoes was coming to serve us but they seen that, thumper (gun) hanging out of my seat cushion. The bitch jumped out and bought two bags." Nine added chuckling.

"Blood, that's the bitch I dumped on. We were at the light on Rosecrans and Stanford on our way back to the hood. We look on the other side of the street, these hoes trying to get active chucking up the bookie (Crip sign) out the window blood. So I bust a C.K. and pulls on the passenger side and start dumping on the bitch. The bitch in the backseat of the Brougham got active on us and started busting back; So Tina-ru hung out the window like a mad man and ate they ass up." Vanity explained, catching her breath.

"Is that gun loaded?" asked Nine

"Hell yeah." Responded Tina-ru. "We bout to go C.K. riding blood."

"On who?" Asked Solomon. "Do y'all know where them crab bitches were from?"

"Nawh, them bitches kept screaming Bompton rip (Compton Crip) blood, Smurf added, becoming upset at what just happened. Smurf is five foot four, one hundred and fifteen pounds. In the face, she's hard on the eyes but her body is banging. Her hair is short but she keeps it in a finger wave hair style.

"Shit, we just gone hit all of em."

"Blood! Blood! There goes that van homie! Hey y'all look out blood!" Nine shouted, to all his Piru comrades.

All the females turned towards the van that's about to make a left turn onto the block from Towne Avenue. Tina-ru jacks off the .380 putting one in the chamber. Nine grabs his 9mm off his lap, while Solomon grabs the AR-15 and takes it off safety, slowly walking to the end of the driveway preparing for a gun battle.

The van cruises onto the block distracting the Piru members. The Crips timed this attack with precision.

"Was'sup blood? What that Piru like nigga?!" Tina-ru shouted, as the van slowly passed by them.

As they watch the van, a brown four door Nova creeps onto the block firing over ten rounds from a tech-nine semi-automatic and a street sweeper 12 gauge.

Smurf and Kay-Kay get hit in the arm, hand and leg, falling onto the pavement moaning. Vanity ducks down and runs to her jeep opening the passenger side driver's seat and got active. Tina-ru uses the hood of the jeep for cover exchanging fire with the Crips in the brown vehicle, hitting one of the shooters in the face. His tech nine falls out the car into the street.

Nine purposely leaps from the wheel chair onto the pavement so he wouldn't be a sitting duck. He fired several rounds at the back tires but was unsuccessful.

Solomon fired several rounds at the vehicle knocking out the side and back windshield. The Caprice mashed down the block heading towards San Pedro Street.

Smurf and Kay-Kay remained lying on the sidewalk in pain.

"Blood! Everybody bool?" Asked Solomon, walking towards Nine helping him back into his chair.

"I'm bool." Nine answered.

"Blood! I'm hit." Smurf replied, calmly still lying onto the pavement.

"Me too homie" Kay-Kay added lying several inches from her.

Alright, hold up." responded Tina-ru Solomon noticed the same 83 Fleetwood Brougham hitting the corner. "Blood! Watch out for them crab bitches!" yelled Solomon. Before he could raise the AR-15, two females hung out of the vehicle's passenger and backseat window, letting the Pirus have it once again.

Tina-ru knocked Nine back onto the pavement and laid on top of him as a shield firing her last couple of rounds at the automobile.

As the car passed, Solomon ran into the middle of the street and unloaded. He knocked out the back windshield, hitting the right side back tire causing the Cadillac to swerve out of control down the block.

With that much activity the police were bound to hit the block in a matter of minutes. Solomon and Tina-ru grabbed Nine placing him back into his wheel chair. Tina-ru quickly pushed Nine into the backyard.

"Blood, I'mma mash out. I got this heat on me." said Vanity, jumping into the jeep, speeding off down the block.

"Smurf, Kay-Kay, I'mma call the paramedics for y'all, but I got to stash this rifle first, before One Time (police) comes." Solomon explained.

"Alright homie, handle your business. We bool." Smurf replied, still lying on the pavement.

September 18, 1987   Friday 2:40 p.m.

FIVE

Solomon strolled into his history class ten minutes late and quietly sat down at his desk. Mrs. Milano is at the chalkboard giving her version of genetic make-up, while eyeing Solomon with a straight face, appearing to be upset; but deep down inside she was happy as hell to see him.

"Can someone in the classroom tell me anything concerning genetics?" asked Mrs. Milano, taking a seat at her desk. She looked throughout the classroom waiting for an answer. All the students looked at each other dumbfounded.

"Nobody can give you an answer Mrs. Milano, Centennial High School has the lowest test scores in the state of California," said Solomon, twirling his three-karat diamond in his ear.

"Is that true Solomon? Where did you get that information from?" she asked out of concern.

"Yes, it is true. I read it in the Los Angeles Times." he responded, sitting up in his chair. "But to answer your question. According to the dictionary, genetics is the branch of biology that deals with heredity and variation in similar or related animals and plants. But the answer I think you're looking for is, the genetic features or constitution of an individual, group or kind," he replied.

Smart ass! Mrs. Milano thought to herself.

Solomon formed a smirk on his face. "Would you like for me to give an example?"

Mrs. Milano smiled before answering. "Please, do so."

"Well, I'mma use myself as an example. Africans have dominant genes and whites have recessive genes. If you take a black man and a white woman and they have a child, it's going to be born black and vice versa," Solomon explained.

A student in the row next to Solomon raises his hand.

"Yes, Mr. Watkins, do you have a question for me, or Solomon?"

"I have a question for Solomon Miss," the student responded.

Solomon turned towards the student. "Was'sup, homie?"

"I don't know what dominant or recessive means. Can you explain?" asked the student, putting Solomon on the spot; so he thinks.

Solomon walks up to the chalkboard grabbing the eraser. "Do you mind?" he asked Mrs. Milano, erasing the board.

"No Solomon, I don't mind," Mrs. Milano replied, eager to see what he's about to present to the classroom.

Solomon writes both words on the chalkboard and behind each word, he gives the definition. "You guys need to take a note of this, so you won't forget it," he stated, like a professor in college. Every student grabs a pen and some paper, jotting down the information. "Always remember you guys, dominant means: ruling, dominating and prevailing. Recessive means: receding or tending to recede, which means becoming less," Solomon explained, placing the piece of chalk, onto the chalk holder, that's attached to the board. "Example, I'm a mixture of Black, Asian and White."

"Mmmph, mmph, mmph!" Tina-ru interrupted out loud.

"Ms. Lucas, that's not appropriate at this time," said Mrs. Milano, with a look of seriousness on her face. "Continue Solomon."

Solomon chuckled at the females. "If you look at my facial features and skin tone, you can see which gene is dominant. My hair for some reason, black people think that this is good hair. It's not, its bad hair. It has no strength, it can't stand on its own. I can't wear an afro; this is my recessive gene. My skin tone has hue in it, that's my dominant gene," Solomon explained proudly.

The school bell rung, all the students gathered up their materials and exited the classroom.

"Solo, let's roll blood," demanded Tina-ru, who is at the door, watching Solomon as he lingers around the classroom.

"Alright," Solomon responded, slapping on his Pittsburg Pirate's baseball cap.

"Um, Solomon, I need to have a word with you, please," Mrs. Milano pleaded. She knew that she had more pull with Solomon, than Tina-ru did and had no problem with rubbing it in her face. Once again she looks at Tina-ru. "Alone."

Solomon turned towards Tina-ru smiling. "I'mma catch up with you later homie," he stated.

Tina-ru became upset and slammed the door of the classroom.

Solomon and Mrs. Milano burst into laughter.

"Hmmph, I see someone has an attitude." replied Mrs. Milano

"Why do you agitate that girl like that?"

"Maybe she's agitating me. Have you ever thought about that?"

Solomon hunched his shoulders. "To each his own."

"I liked your presentation earlier concerning genetics." said Mrs. Milano.

Solomon agreed. "Thank you…. How many kids do you have Mrs. Milano?"

"I don't have any. Why?"

"I want you to adopt me," Solomon responded, with a straight look on his face.

Mrs. Milano blushed.

"I'm serious," he shot back.

"I don't think that will be a good idea, Solomon."

"I'm too young to be your boyfriend, I'm not even legal yet. You'll go to jail for statutory rape," said Solomon, smiling profusely.

"I'm married Solomon, I'm not looking for a boyfriend."

"Have you ever cheated on your husband?"

"No"

"Will you?"

Mrs. Milano rested her chin inside her palm in deep thought.

"It's taking you too long to answer, so there's doubt."

Mrs. Milano looked at her wrist watch. "I must leave Solomon. I have a few errands to run," she explained, grabbing her coat and purse.

"Can you give me a ride home?"

"What happened to that car that you were driving?"

"Um, it wasn't mine, I was borrowing it."

"Yes, I'll give you a ride, come on. "They exited the classroom, walking to the teachers' parking lot, getting inside a black, 1988 500SL Mercedes Benz.

"You make enough to buy a Benz on a teacher's salary?" asked Solomon, placing on his seat belt.

"I have other business ventures outside of my regular job, Solomon."

"Like what?" asked a nosy Solomon.

"Real estate, maybe if you'll be around in a couple of years, I can show you a thing or two."

"Oh, I'm quite sure you could show me a lot of things." Solomon answered sarcastically, as the Mercedes sped out of the parking lot, heading west on El Segundo Blvd.

"Where do you live Solomon?"

"Um, make a left at the light on Avalon, then a right on a one hundred and twenty-ninth," Solomon instructed.

Three minutes later, the Benz makes a right on 129th Street. Solomon searches the block, but for some reason, no one is hanging out. They pass his residence, reaching the corner of 129th and Towne Avenue.

"Where to now?"

"Make a left right here, then a left on a 130th street." Solomon instructed.

Mrs. Milano does so. In the middle of the block, there are over fifteen Pirus hanging out selling crack, drinking Thunderbird, smoking weed and slap boxing. Solomon smiles, amongst the group is Tina-ru, sitting on the hood of a burgundy 1987' Chevy Iroc.

"These are your friends Solomon?" asked Mrs. Milano, driving slowly down the street frowning; as she observes the thugs, indulging in their everyday activities.

"Yeah pull over in front of this burgundy Iroc," Solomon ordered.

Mrs. Milano and Tina-ru makes eye contact. Tina-ru turns her lip up at the teacher, as she pulls alongside of the curb. "Oh, I see. You wanted me to drop you off to your girlfriend?"

Solomon laughed, because she figured out his scheme. "Nawh, you know that's not my girlfriend."

The Pirus stopped horse playing and keyed in on Solomon and Mrs. Milano.

"Okay, Mr. Spencer. I guess I'll see you in class Monday," said Mrs. Milano extending her hand out to his.

Solomon shakes her hand in return. "Alright, I'll see you Monday." he replied, climbing out of the vehicle, watching as she drives off the block.

"You and that teacher seems pretty tight...Y'all hanging out after school on the regular. Now she's dropping you off on the block? Whuut... excuse me playa." Tina-ru stated, in a singing voice, jealous of their friendship. She's starting to develop a deep hatred for Mrs. Milano, for fucking with her man.

Solomon sits on the hood of the Iroc. "We don't have anything going on, trust me."

"Hmmph." responded Tina-ru, rolling her eyes with her lip curled up.

Solomon pays her no mind, as he acknowledges his fellow Piru comrades, giving them half hugs and handshakes.

"One Time!" someone shouted, from the corner. Before they could do anything, the gang task force was already rolling up on them three deep, with their doors opened.

The driver threw the gear in park, while it was slowing down, causing the vehicle to jerk, before stopping.

Three officers jumped out of the car with aggression, demanding all the Pirus to place their hands on the hood of their patrol car. Eight of the fifteen Pirus that were hanging in the front yard took off running, into the house or backyard because of illegal contraband in their possession. Officers refuse to give chase.

Two of the officers patted the gang members down for weapons and narcotics but came up empty handed.

"You guys better not be hanging out too much, the Compton Crips will be through here in a minute. I don't wanna come back and this block is taped off and you guys are laid out," said Officer Milano, rocking from hill to toe.

"Yeah, we heard they came through here letting y'all have it last week." Esson responded, snickering.

The Pirus remained silent. They didn't feed into the pig's reverse psychology. After shaking them down and running their names for warrants, the officers released them and drove off.

"Man, I'm glad I didn't have no pistol on me. I would've been hit, the way they hit that corner a minute ago, blood. On Piru." Solomon expressed, relieved.

Moments later, all the Pirus are posted back up to where they were, resuming normal activity. Out of nowhere, a rush of clients for crack cocaine floods the block, arriving on feet, bicycles and in vehicles. This goes on for ten minutes straight.

A 1986, tan four door Caprice Classic, cruises by the Pirus, with three occupants inside. The automobile cruises by the Pirus unnoticed, except for Solomon, who is eyeing the suspicious vehicle, as it turns into a driveway, making its way back down the block.

"Blood, where's the jammy at? Hurry up!" demanded a nervous Solomon, walking towards the front yard where majority of the Pirus are standing.

A Piru meets Solomon at the gate with a .357 Python and hands it to him.

"Blood, watch this tan car! Get out the street fool!" Tina-ru shouted.

The Pirus quickly got out the street, posting up behind parked cars, for cover. The Pirus frown at the vehicle, as it slowly passes by.

Gunfire erupts out of nowhere. The Pirus scatter in all directions to avoid being shot. Solomon lets off one round at the tan Caprice, but gunshots are being fired from somewhere else. The Caprice sped off the block. The shooting stops, Solomon looks at the corner and sees a man fleeing on foot up Towne Avenue, jumping into a vehicle and speeding off.

"Blood, that's the second time something like that done happened!"

Solomon vented. "Enough is enough, fuck that, we bout to get active!"

"Yeah, blood, this shit is getting out of hand, homie...for real," Tina-ru responded, reaching into her pocket pulling out a set of car keys. "Come on, let's go hit a few corners, blood." They both jumped into the burgundy Iroc with a pistol and sped off into traffic.

*****

Tina-ru and Solomon cruised through a neighborhood known as T-zone, a Crip set that sits on the Compton/Gardena borderline. They cruised through every block, not a Crip in sight. They drove on the other side of San Pedro Street, through a hood known as Tragnu Park. After cruising every street, they still came up with nothing.

"Where these fools at blood?" Tina-ru asked, becoming irritated of the mission.

"Man, your guess is just as good as mine, homie. I don't know where these fools could be at. Go on the east side of Bompton," Solomon demanded.

They drove east, on Compton Boulevard, until they got to Willowbrook Avenue. They looked over to their right, at the shopping plaza and couldn't believe their eyes.

"Ba-loood! Look at all them crabs, homie...damn them fools are deep as hell!" Solomon responded, in disbelief, looking at what appeared to be well over two hundred Compton Crips, dressed in blue attire, from head to toe.

"I'mma bust a C.K. (U-turn) and drive by Bompton (Compton) High School. This is where all these fools are at, they're having a meeting, blood," replied Tina-ru, making a U-turn in the other direction, then making a left on Aprilla Street. Both sides of the street are filled with Compton Crips. The presence of the police is also felt, being that Compton High School is located directly across the street from the police precinct. The police patrol the area in cars, bikes and foot.

"Blood, One Time is too thick, let's catch some crabs lingering behind," said Solomon, looking around nervously, at the Crips and cops.

"Yeah, you right," Tina-ru responded, turning on the nearest side street, ending up on Compton Boulevard, driving west. They reach Wilmington Avenue and turn into a neighborhood known as 'Palmer Block' Compton Crips.

"Aw Blood, there go One Time," said Tina-ru, sitting up in her seat. The police car is cruising slow, coming in her direction. As they pass each other, both police look into their vehicle. Tina-ru and Solomon looked straight ahead, trying not to look at the cops, which raised suspicion with the authorities. The police sped up and turned into the nearest driveway, to turn their vehicle around, so they can stop the burgundy Iroc.

Solomon was glued to the mirror on the passenger side. His heart pounds out of control, as he sees the police turning around. "Blood, Bone out. Here they come."

Tina-ru steps on the gas, speeding down Dwight Street, until she reaches Rosecrans Avenue, making a left turn. The police speeds up, trailing the Iroc from a distance. The Iroc makes a sharp right on Parmalee, pushing the speed to eighty-five miles per hour. The Iroc makes a left turn on Piru Street, coming to a complete stop. Tina-ru and Solomon bells out of the vehicle, running in separate directions.

Solomon runs in-between two houses, with gun in hand, hopping the gate, running through several backyards until he reaches one hundred and thirty-third street. He can hear the police vehicle zooming up the block on a hundred and thirty-second street, which is around the corner. Solomon crawls underneath a 79' Monte Carlo that's parked in the driveway and sits still. Moments later, the ghetto bird hovers over the vicinity. Solomon closes his eyes and pray.

*****

"Freeze!" both officers yelled, jumping out the car with guns drawn, at Tina-ru. "Put your hands up now! Put em up you fucking scum bag!"

Tina-ru does so, coming to a complete stop, dropping to her knees.

The police slaps the cuffs on her and makes her sit on the curb, until they call for a female officer to pat her down.

"Who was the person that jumped out of the passenger's side?" asked the officer.

"What passenger?" asked a dumb founded Tina-ru. "I don't know what you're talking about blood."

"Oh, you wanna be tough? I'm going to send you to Silva Brand and see how tough you are," said the officer, all in Tina-ru's face.

"Do what you gotta do, I don't give a fuck" she responded calmly.

"Oh, don't worry smart ass. I will," said the officer.

Thirty minutes later, a female officer arrives to the scene and searched Tina-ru, coming up with nothing. After police searched the Iroc, they still came up empty handed. The female officer then searched the vehicle, taking longer than usual. After twenty minutes of picking and prying, she steps out the vehicle with a half-ounce of rock cocaine. She holds the bag of narcotics into the air. "Got it."

Tina-ru is placed in the back of the police car and sent to the Carson Sheriff's station.

*****

Solomon woke up startled, bumping his head on the muffler of the Monte Carlo. Night time has fallen and he has no clue as to what time it is or the whereabouts of the police. Slowly he crawls from underneath the car with pistol in hand, walking to the edge of the driveway, to get a view of the street in both directions. He tucked the pistol in his waist, covered it up with his shirt and walked down the street towards Central Avenue. He gets to the corner, looking both ways before crossing. He finds a break in the traffic and dashes across. As soon as he gets to the other side of the street, he is startled by the revving engine of a police car. Solomon bolts down the sidewalk, running in-between two houses and hopping a fence, dashing through someone's backyard. Two sheriffs jump out of the automobile and give chase.

As Solomon ran, he snatched the gun from his waist and hurled it, as hard as he could. He continued to run hopping fences, until he ended up on Bellhaven Street. Solomon is exhausted; he kneels on the side of a house, to catch his breath. He hears an officer coming through the backyard of the house he's in front of and runs again. As he crosses the street, he almost gets hit by a police car zooming down the street, with their lights off. The officer inside jumps out with flashlight in one hand and a pistol in the other.

"Freeze! You fucking dirt bag, before I shoot!" yelled the officer. Solomon came to a complete stop, throwing his hands into the air.

"Don't make me do it you cocksucker!" shouted the officer, as he nervously inched closer to Solomon. "Drop to your knees and place your hands-on top of your head! Now! You asshole!"

Solomon does so. Moments later the other cop arrives to the scene breathing heavily. "How come you ran earlier?" he asked Solomon, fighting for air.

"I don't know what you're talking about," Solomon responded, his asshole tightened out of fear, hoping they don't find the gun.

"Cuff his ass up and put him in the backseat, while we go back and search the area," the officer demanded, still fighting for air as he back tracked.

"10-four," the other cop replied, by taking his order placing Solomon in the backseat. Afterwards, the cop pulled his flashlight from his belt and joined his fellow officer in the backyard.

Solomon exhaled, leaning his head up against the window, closing his eyes. Two minutes later, his meditation was interrupted by the knocking on the window. A startled Solomon opened his eyes, taking his head off the window. It took his equilibrium a moment to register the face. A five foot-nine, brown skinned man, with a Phillies baseball cap and burgundy clothing is at the window. Solomon smiles, this is Hot-dog from West Side Piru, 134th street.

"Solo, what's up blood? You trying to get out of there?" asked Hot-dog, looking over both of his shoulders for the police.

"On Piru, open the door blood," Solomon responded, excitedly.

Hot-dog pulls the sleeve of his burgundy sweat shirt, over his hand and lifts the chrome latch freeing Solomon from bondage.

"Come on Blood, D-dog is over there in the car, waiting," said Hot-dog. They both jogged over to the '68 Chevy Impala, that was waiting with the lights out. Hot-dog opened the passenger's side door, lifting the front seat. Solomon dove in head first, landing in the back seat, with cuffs still on. Hot-dog closes the door, the Impala cruises off quietly. Ten minutes later, the officers arrived back to the scene, empty handed. They were already pissed, from not finding nothing, after realizing that Solomon has somehow escaped, is now a personal issue between them and the Pirus. They jumped in the patrol car and caught a Piru walking alone, on Central Avenue and Rosecrans Boulevard. They roughed him up, then dropped him off in a Crip territory known as the Park Village Crips. Thirty minutes later, the Pirus body was found on Alondra Boulevard, riddled with bullets.

OCTOBER 2, 1987   Friday 5:30 p.m.

SIX

Two weeks has gone by and Solomon has been staying in the house during the day and only coming out at night, to avoid the police since that night he eluded them.

Solomon is in the living room ironing his burgundy khaki shirt, listening to 'Hurry up this way again', by the Stylistics. Chinadoll comes from her bedroom, into the living room, with a Newport hanging from in-between her lips and a can of beer in her hand. She stops by the front door and stares at Solomon, trying to figure out what he is up to.

"I noticed you've been in the house for the past two weeks during the day. Who are you hiding from?" asked Chinadoll, taking a long pull off the cigarette, watching Solomon through the smoke, occasionally sipping from the beer.

"I'm not hiding from no one," Solomon responded.

"You're a mutha-fucking lie fool! You're hiding from somebody nigga and you need to let me know who it is. I don't want any unexpected visits. You can't fool me blood. I've been a Piru before you were even thought of," China responded, taking another drag off the Newport.

"You right," said Solomon.

"What?!" Chinadoll asked, with an attitude. "What you say fool?!"

"I said you're right, momma," he responded, removing his shirt from the ironing board putting it on.

"You still haven't answered my fucking question, blood," Chinadoll stated.

"I was running from the police and got caught. They put me in the back of the car and started searching for the gun that I threw in somebody's backyard. Some homies happen to drive by and see me and let me out, then gave me a ride to the hood," Solomon explained.

Chinadoll stared at him not blinking. "You and who?"

"Tina-ru," he responded.

"Tina-ru?" Chinadoll asked, confused. "Who in the hell is Tina-ru? That little ugly gal around the corner?"

"Yeah, she lives on 130th." he replied.

"I know who she is. What was y'all going to do?"

"Put some work in on some rips," he replied looking her straight in the eyes.

"I don't believe your ass. You too soft, you ain't got it in you to be no Piru," China responded, unaware of her son's reputation with the Pirus.

Solomon's feelings were crushed, but he played it off by smiling, pissing his mother off. "I'm just like you, when you were my age."

Chinadoll went on the defense, shaking her head in disagreement. "Nawh, nawh little nigga you're nothing like me when I was your age. I got two hot ones (murders) under my belt, on some Mona's." (Mona Park Crips) she explained, walking to the front door, thumping the remainder of the cigarette into the grass, returning to the living room, placing the can of beer on the table.

Solomon was happy inside. Even though they're having a dispute, they're having a conversation, and to Solomon, this was a start to a mother and son relationship. Never, in his seventeen years of living, have they talked this much. Just when things seem to be going good, Kyle walks into the living room rubbing his eyes, waking up from a power nap.

"Kyle, rush that fool, blood. He's faking the funk, on the nasty dunk," China demanded, without hesitation Kyle ran up on Solomon throwing a two-piece, catching him on the side of his face, causing him to fall into the ironing board knocking over the hot iron, which fell onto the floor, inches from his face.

Kyle stopped allowing Solomon to get up.

"Blood, you almost burnt my face fool," Solomon responded, becoming furious as he stood up.

"Why you conversing fool? Get active!" Chinadoll shouted to Kyle, while firing up another cigarette.

On demand, Kyle rushed Solomon once again, swinging wildly. Solomon didn't want to hurt his brother, so he grabbed him around his waist, picked him up into the air and slammed him onto the floor hard.

Chinadoll looked on disappointed at Kyle, who lied on his side shaking his head, bringing himself back into consciousness.

"I don't wanna hurt you blood, get up," Solomon responded backing away from him.

"I wish Maurice was here, he would've served your ass," China boasted. "On Piru blood!"

"Nawh, I doubt it. What I gotta do to prove to you, that I ain't to be messed with?" Solomon asked his mother sincerely.

"Who you talking to fool? You ain't cut like that. Get outta my damn face, fool. Now!" Chinadoll shouted, pointing her finger towards the door.

Solomon formed a devilish smirk on his face as he walked out the door, into the front yard.

"Muthafucka," China responded underneath her breath, soon after taking the last sip of beer from the can on the table. She looked over at Kyle, who was getting off the ground. "You're starting to really piss me off dog for real. Get your mark ass up and go back to your room."

Solomon looked west watching the sunset, enjoying the various colors the sky is reflecting. His enjoyment is interrupted by Mrs. Milano pulling alongside the curb in front of him. Solomon cannot believe his eyes. He watches as the window goes down on the driver side, revealing her sexy face.

"How you doing Mr. Spencer?" asked Mrs. Milano with a huge smile on her face. "Long time no see. I had to come and check on you."

"Hey, how you doing Mrs. Milano?" Solomon responded, with a huge smile on his face.

"Are you busy?"

"Nawh, I was just about to step out for a minute," said Solomon.

"Come on, let's take a little ride. I would like to talk to you, it could be beneficial," Mrs. Milano explained.

"Alright," said Solomon, exiting the front yard, climbing into the car.

Chinadoll stood in the doorway and watched as her son drove off with his school teacher.

*****

Solomon inhaled the strong cherry aroma, inside Mrs. Milano's 500SL, that came from her air fresheners. She glanced over at Solomon, blushing, as he nods his head to 'Sweet Dreams', by the Eurhythmics.

"Do you listen to a variety of music Solomon?"

"Yes...How about you?"

"I listen to everything, except for some rap," Mrs. Milano responded.

"Oh yeah? Why not?"

"Um, the beats are interesting. I think it's more of the lyrical content that I disagree with," she replied. "I like Run D.M.C. I have the Raising Hell album."

"So, you're saying a rapper must be saying something interesting, for you to listen?"

"Yes, pretty much."

"When you get a chance, listen to Boogie Down Productions or Eric B. & Rakim," Solomon responded, turning the radio dial to AM stereo 1580 KDAY. The song 'Criminal Minded,' by Boogie Down Productions is playing.

Solomon nods his head, to the song. "Here we go right here. This is Boogie Down Productions," Mrs. Milano smiles profusely, as she turns onto the Harbor freeway, heading north.

"Where are we going, if you don't mind me asking?" asked Solomon.

"On a date," replied Mrs. Milano.

"Oh yeah?" asked Solomon, out of excitement. "How come I couldn't get dressed up like you?"

"Dressed up? I'm not dressed up, Solomon" she responded, smiling.

Solomon eye fucks Mrs. Milano from head to toe stopping at her chest, enjoying the cleavage shot. "Yeah right, you're not dressed up. You have on black high heels, matching dress slacks and a silk shirt, with shades sitting on top of your head and you're not dressed up? Stop playing. You look nice though."

"Thank you, Solomon," responded Mrs. Milano, smiling. She reached over and playfully squeezed his left leg, with her right hand. "You look nice also, Mr. Spencer."

Solomon's dick instantly filled with blood, almost touching her hand. "Mrs. Milano touching me is not appropriate, ma'am," he responded sarcastically.

Mrs. Milano snatched her hand away from his leg. "I apologize Solomon."

They both burst into laughter.

"Mrs. Milano, if you don't mind me asking, what is your first name?"

"Christina, only when we are alone, never in the classroom," she explained, pointing her finger at him.

"It is also not polite to point your finger at someone, too," he responded.

"I'm not kidding Solomon, don't ever call me by my name in class, only when we're alone," she repeated, still pointing.

Solomon smiled. "You plan on being with me alone, more than once?"

She placed her hand back onto the steering wheel. "Yes."

Solomon looked out the passenger's window, smiling. "What about your husband, Christina?"

"What about him?"

"What is he gonna think?"

"Don't worry about him, he's always working," she shot back.

"What's his occupation? If you don't mind me asking."

"He's in law enforcement," she responded.

Solomon reached over to the car stereo and turned the dial to 102.3 KJLH. 'Sunshine,' by Alexander O'Neal is playing. "You like that?" He asked looking at her.

"Yes," she replied, firmly.

The two listened to the radio in silence, until they reached their destination, which took about thirty minutes.

They arrived at a restaurant called 'The Hungry Tiger,' in West Hollywood.

After valet parking, they both sat at a table that was reserved specifically for them.

"What are you ordering?" asked Mrs. Milano, looking over the menu.

"Steak well done, shrimp and salad," Solomon responded, "And yourself?"

"I'm not sure yet," she replied then ten seconds later, she placed the menu on the table.

"I have someone I want you to meet. He is a friend of mine, that's doing a documentary on gangs in Los Angeles. I thought that you'll be the perfect person to talk to being that you're a gang member, who is also highly intelligent," explained Mrs. Milano.

"I'm cool with that, maybe this will be a stepping stone for my acting and directing, career," said Solomon.

"Yes, that's true," she responded.

"Hi, are you guys ready to order?" asked the waitress.

"Yes. I would like the Dungeness crab and a salad," Mrs. Milano replied, handing the waitress the menu. "Thank you."

"You're welcome. And what would you like, sir," the waitress asked Solomon.

"I would like the garlic noodles and a salad please, thank you," Solomon replied, handing her the menu.

"You're welcome," responded the waitress, flashing a million-dollar smile at Solomon. Mrs. Milano sees it and starts frowning.

"So, when am I gonna meet your friend?"

"Maybe sometime next week. I had to make sure that you were okay with it, first," Mrs. Milano responded.

"Oh, yeah, I'm definitely okay with it."

"Well, there you have it, as soon as I get in touch with him, I'll notify you, so you guys can hook up," she explained.

Twenty minutes later, the waitress returns with both plates. They both enjoyed their meals and each other's company. Afterwards, she drove around the West Hollywood and Hollywood Hills area, showing him some of her rental properties. Solomon was impressed with the estates and told her that one day he would like to own some real estate. She smiled in return, agreeing to assist him with anything he needed.

October 3, 1987   Saturday 12:02 a.m.

SEVEN

Mrs. Milano pulls into Skate Land U.S.A. and cruises to the back-parking lot, which is the front entrance for patrons. The parking lot is congested with customized: Nissan trucks, Toyota trucks, Suzuki Jeeps, El Camino trucks, K-5 Blazers, Cadillacs, Regals, Cutlasses and Low Riders. Mrs. Milano looked on in awe, of all the bright red: baseball caps, t-shirts, khaki pants, tennis shoes and a blanket size bandana, that the Bloods are walking through the parking lot with, waving in the air forcefully.

"You know all these people, Solomon?"

"Yeah majority of them"

"Do you think you can get all of them in the documentary?"

"Oh yeah, if you come on a night like this."

"How do I get out of here?"

Solomon pointed with his finger. "Just make a complete circle around these parked cars," said Solomon, she does so and pulls to the front entrance. "Well Christina, this is it."

"Yes Solomon, it is. I had a pretty interesting dinner date with you tonight."

"Yes, I did too and thank you for the dinner, the documentary job and the ride here. I appreciate it," Solomon expressed.

"Hold on," said Mrs. Milano, reaching into the backseat grabbing her Anne Klein purse, placing it in her lap and opening it.

She pulled out a crispy fifty-dollar bill from her coin purse and handed it to him.

"Thank you, I appreciate it," responded Solomon, accepting the legal tender.

"Yeah, I don't want you to go out there and start selling drugs for extra money and get yourself caught up. We need you to stick around, so you can do the film," explained Mrs. Milano, taking her finger and tapping it on her tongue wetting it, getting the cold out the corner of Solomon's eyes.

"Thank you," Solomon replied, getting a hard on from her touch.

"You're welcome," she responded reaching over, giving him a hug.

Mixed emotions went through Solomon's mind, body and soul. He felt loved, horny and abused all at the same time. He exited the vehicle and watched as she drove off.

"Solo, what's up Piru?" asked Hot-dog, walking towards him in an all red khaki suit and matching Chuck Taylor tennis shoes. The two exchanged handshakes.

"Ain't shit blood, just bickin it. What's popping for tonight?" asked Solomon.

"Shit, I don't know. Me and D-dog might go C-kaying (Crip killing) tonight, we'll see," Hot-dog responded.

"What's going on inside there?" Solomon asked, nodding his head towards the skating rink.

"Man, it's a gang of hoes in there sweating out their basket weaves. Other than that, the same ole shit," Hot-dog replied. "You wanna bell inside?"

"Yeah, let's slide in for a minute," said Solomon.

The two pay at the window and gets patted down by the security guards, before entering. Solomon and Hot-dog walks through the crowd of gang members that's dressed in all red and burgundy attire. All the men are standing around nodding their heads to the pounding beats, while the women dance with each other in separate groups.

"Hey homie, I'll be back. I'mma go and holler at this little broad by the snack bar," said Hot-dog, walking off, disappearing in the sea of people.

Solomon walked over by the D.J. booth and posted up on the rail, overlooking the dance floor.

"Solo! Solo! Was'sup blood?" Yelled an excited Tina-ru, running up on him, giving him a bear hug.

"When did you get out, blood?" asked Solomon, smiling profusely.

"Two days ago, I was in Buena Park over my sister's house getting my shit together. That day we ran from the police, them fools found some dope in my car, and took me down," explained Tina-ru, leaning up against the rail beside Solomon.

"I ran and hid underneath a parked car, in somebody's driveway and fell asleep. When I woke up it was dark, so I started walking to the hood. Then out of nowhere, One Time swooped up on me on Central, so I broke hopping gates through different backyards. I slung the pistol as hard as I could, then another police caught me on Belhaven, then put me in the car and left. The homie Hot-dog let me out the backseat, then gave me a ride to the hood," Solomon explained.

Damn blood, you lucky as hell. Have you been going to school?"

"Hell nawh, Mrs. Milano came through the hood earlier looking for me," Solomon bragged.

Tina-ru frowned. "She came to the hood blood?"

Solomon nodded his head in agreement. "Yeah, she dropped me off up here about ten minutes ago."

"Blood, what's up with y'all two? You doing something with that lady?" Tina-ru stated, getting upset, folding her arms against her chest.

"Nawh, she hooked me up with this dude that's doing a documentary," Solomon replied.

"I think she wants you to pimp her. She comes looking for you in the hood, then gets you a job that can make you famous and drop you off at the skating rink? That's pimping to me. I wouldn't be surprised if she gave you some money, when she dropped you off," Tina-ru explained.

Solomon burst out laughing at her preciseness. "Blood, you buck wild."

"Nawh fool, you know I'm right," she shot back. "What you doing when the skating rink closes?" Solomon hunched his shoulders. "Nothing. Why?"

"Let's get a room I'm paying," said Tina-ru.

"How come we have to wait until the skating rink is over with? What's wrong with going now?" asked Solomon, still horny from Mrs. Milano's touch earlier.

Tina-ru ·grabbed Solomon by the arm tight and led him out the skating rink.

*****

The Ramada Inn on Artesia Boulevard, right off Figueroa Street, is a low key motel that every gang member in L.A. County has discovered.

Solomon waits inside of Tina-ru's vehicle, until she gives him the word. Five minutes later, she waves at him, letting him know that everything is good. Solomon climbs out of the automobile trailing behind Tina-ru, who has already entered room 204 on the second floor.

Tina-ru is laying across the bed on her stomach, when Solomon entered the room closing the door behind him. He climbs onto the bed, lying on her back and starts playfully grinding on her voluptuous ass. She throws her ass back at Solomon. That makes him grind harder, causing friction almost starting a fire.

"Don't you think it'll be better, if you take my pants off?" asked Tina-ru, still throwing her ass at him.

Solomon stood up and removed all his clothing, except for his burgundy high top Chuck Taylors. Tina-ru quickly removed all her clothes and threw them in the corner. Her smooth cocoa skin tone and figure is flawless. In the face, she resembles the actress

Kim Fields, when she played "Tootie," from the television show, Facts of Life.

Her body boasts a 38-24-38, hour glass shape, with a washboard stomach that's chiseled to perfection. The only turn off is, her nappy haired pussy.

"Come to the edge of the bed," demanded Solomon, stroking his eight and half inch mushroom head schlong.

Tina-ru does so staring at his tally whacker. She then began circling the-head of his cock with her tongue for several revolutions before putting all his dick inside her mouth. She grabbed both of his butt cheeks and pulled him inside her mouth until she gagged. Solomon was in heaven. Tina-ru turned it up a notch by pulling his dick from her mouth and spitting on it, then devoured his love log until he moaned and pulled away from her out of ecstasy.

"I want you to fuck me, like you fantasize about fucking our teacher," Tina-ru replied, lying on her back placing her knees against her chest.

"Why you got to use our teacher as an example?" stated Solomon, as he slowly fits the tip of his dick inside her warm pussy.

"I watch you guys' eye contact. The eyes never lie," Tina-ru responded being sarcastic. On that note, Solomon batter rammed his pipe inside her.

"Ssss-ouuucch! You're trying to hurt me fool."

Solomon pinned her knees to her chest with his hands and vigorously pounded her love box causing her to scream and holler like someone was assaulting her. After stroking her in this position for three minutes, the funk from her pussy lingered into the air of the room. Solomon pulled out. "Lay on your stomach."

Tina-ru declined his command, getting into a doggy style position. "Fuck me this way, blood."

Without saying a word, he grabbed her by the waist and guided his dick inside of her sloppy wet love nest. The splashing sound of her cunt became louder, as he sped up his stroking pace. Tina-ru moaned in ecstasy. The pussy was so good, he grabbed a handful of braids with both hands and started pulling and fucking her harder at the same time. He banged her like this for several minutes, until he felt a tingling sensation in his toes. He pulled out.

"Hold up, I'm about to nut," Solomon stated, laying on the edge of the bed.

"Well here, let me ride it so we can both cum at the same time," responded Tina-ru, holding his dick in position mounting on top of it, sliding down slow, taking as much as she can take. "Damn, this dick is good. The teacher is gonna lose her mind when she gets some of this dick."

"What makes you think that I'm going to give her some?" Solomon replied smirking.

"Just like I said. It's in the eyes. The eyes never lie. Plus, a woman knows." Tina-ru responded, slamming herself up and down on his pole with her head held back enjoying the ride. She rode his cock for ten more minutes. "I'm about to cum homie."

Solomon started thrusting his cock, meeting her rhythm Tina-ru pounded her right hand repeatedly into his chest as she felt her orgasm coming.

"Let it out," said Solomon, feeling a tingling sensation in his toes.

"SSSSS-AAAHHH! SSSS-OOOOH-Shit!" cried Tina-ru, as she jerked into ecstasy.

"AAAAGH!" said Solomon, letting out his load inside of her.

Tina-ru pulled off him and laid beside him, stroking his semi-hard meat stick. "So, where do we go from here?" asked Tina-ru, already falling in love with Solomon.

"Back to the hood, shit," responded Solomon, walking into the bathroom cleaning himself off with a hot soapy towel and water. After he cleans himself, he brings her a soapy hot face towel. "Here, get yourself together."

Tina-ru does so, grabbing the towel, digging inside her pussy. Soon after, she entered the bathroom to take a quick shower.

Solomon waited, sitting up on the bed fully dressed, looking at a pornography movie on the television.

Tina-ru steps out of the bathroom in the nude dripping wet, stopping at the foot of the bed. "So, where are you trying to get dropped off, at?"

"Shit, in the hood. Why what's up?"

"Damn homie, I was just trying to kick it with you on some homie time. But you be acting like you're in a rush," Tina-ru responded, forming tears in the wells of her eyes. She was feeling like a 'Wham bam, thank you ma'am.'

Solomon exhaled, he didn't realize he hurt her feelings with his arrogance. "Well, what are you trying to do, Blood?"

"Damn, at least we could spend a night in the room. I mean, I enjoyed the sex, so I don't feel like I wasted my money. But at the same-"

"Alright blood, I feel what you're saying. You don't have to give me an explanation homie," said Solomon, cutting her off. But I do need to go to the hood for a minute to pick up something, then we can come back and kick it."

"Alright, blood," said Tina-ru, putting her clothes back on. Tina-ru was already liking Solomon before the sex, now that he beat those guts up, she's sprung. But she knows she's competing with Mrs. Milano and she felt that he was sprung on her, so she must figure out a way to get Mrs. Milano out the picture. She snatched her car keys off the dresser. "Come on, you ready?"

"Yeah let's bounce," Solomon responded, slowly getting up from the bed.

They both exited the room, jumped in the car and drove north on Avalon Boulevard in silence. Solomon was thinking of how he could ditch Tina-ru, once they made it to the hood. He wasn't feeling being cooped up in that room until checkout time. He glanced at his wrist watch shocked at the time, 2:15 a.m. He figured it was late due to the lack of traffic on the street. The car gets caught at the light on Rosecrans and Avalon. Over at the Shell gas station, Solomon notices an unfamiliar face pumping gas into a Black 83' Coupe de Ville on 14 x 7, gold Dayton wire rims.

"You got a strap?" asked Solomon, looking over at Tina-ru.

Tina-ru is still a little salty at Solomon, because deep in the back of her mind, she knew once they get to the neighborhood, he's gonna elude her. Without saying a word, she reached underneath the dashboard, pulling out a 9mm handgun and hands it to him. She already knew what time it was.

Solomon puts a bullet into the chamber. "Blood, pull into the Shell gas station on the side of that black Coupe."

They both became a little nervous, as they waited for the light. Seconds later, the light turns green, Tina-ru pulls into the gas station and creeps alongside of the Cadillac. Solomon stares at the unfamiliar patron pumping gas into his vehicle. The owner of the Cadillac notices Solomon and identifies himself.

"What's up blood?" inquired the owner of the vehicle, flashing a Blood gang sign at Solomon.

"What's popping blood, where are you from homie?" asked Solomon, still mad dogging the owner of the Cadillac. Just because he uttered the word blood doesn't mean that he's a blood. Most Crips, whenever they get caught slipping, instantaneously convert to a gang that's compatible to the aggressor. This vicinity of Rosecrans and Avalon is a known Blood area. Many Crips outside of the Compton and Carson area have lost their lives at this gas station due to their ignorance of their whereabouts.

"I'm from east side Miller Gangsters, blood," said Syklone who is a caramel colored, six foot-two, two hundred and twenty-five-pound gang banger. He wears his hair in two long braided pony tails on each side, wrapped in red rubber bands that match the laces in his black suede pumas and black short sleeve khaki suit. Syklone walks up to Solomon's side of the vehicle, exposing both of his forearms. Inside both of his arms are blood affiliated tattoos, that reads: 120th street MGB C.K.

The scribe was enough to back up the Miller gangsters claim. Solomon let his guard down. "Alright homie, this West Side Piru. I thought I caught me one slipping, damn."

"That's right blood, that's how you do it homie. If I would've been a crab, I was through," Syklone explained, laughing.

"Oh, without a doubt. Alright homie, I'm headed back to the turf. What they call you blood?" asked Solomon.

"They call me Syklone homie."

"Alright Skye. They call me Solo homie," Solomon responded. "I'll catch up with you at a function or something homie."

"Alright blood."

"Alright blood, be safe," replied Solomon as Tina-ru sped out the gas station, heading north on Avalon Boulevard until they reached a hundred and twenty-ninth street, making a left turn, and drove until they reached Towne Avenue. There are over five Piru members hanging out, selling marijuana, on what is known as the late-night shift. This shift is from midnight, to sunrise.

Tina-ru pulls alongside the curb and turns the engine off. "How long is it going to take you to handle your business, blood?"

"I don't know, I need to holler at the big homie, Nine" Solomon responded, opening the passenger's side of the car climbing out, with pistol in hand. Solomon greeted everyone, but walked up to Nine and gave him a hug. "What's up big homie?"

"Shit, if I had your hands, I'll throw mines away," said Nine, jokingly. "Where are, you coming from, blood?"

"I just came from fucking the shit out of Tina-ru. I should have never did that, cause now she thinks we're a couple or some lame shit like that," Solomon explained, shoving the pistol into his right pocket.

Nine chuckled. "Oh, she's waiting on you now, huh?"

"Yeah, I got to ditch her ass blood."

"Nawh, don't ditch her blood, just tell her to beat it. If you ditch her, it's just gonna make things worse," Nine explained, adjusting both of his legs inside the wheelchair with his hands.

"Yeah, you right. Hold on a minute, homie," said Solomon, walking up to Tina-ru's vehicle, tapping the passenger's side window.

Tina-ru already knew that Solomon was about to put some shit in the game. She rolled the window down with an attitude. "Was'sup blood, you ready to bounce?"

"Hey come back and pick me up in about an hour, blood. Me and the big homie gotta take care of some business," said Solomon, trying his best to think of a good lie.

"An hour?!" Tina-ru shouted. "Blood, it's already two thirty in the morning. Alright I'm cool. Don't trip blood."

"Come back later and get me, then we'll go back to the room and kick it," said Solomon, knowing she wasn't going for that drag.

Tina-ru started up the vehicle, revving up the engine, then burned rubber down the block bringing unnecessary attention to the corner. She knew what she was doing, but didn't give a shit.

Everyone burst out into laughter, including Solomon who walked into the middle of the street watching, as the vehicle did donuts in the middle of San Pedro Street.

"Blood! One Time!" shouted one of his Piru comrades, who was standing in the yard.

A patrol car slowly creeps north on Towne Avenue, then suddenly guns the engine as it makes a left turn onto the block where Solomon is standing, with the headlights off.

"Solo watch out homie!" Nine shouted.

Without looking, Solomon dashed through two parked cars, streaking across the front lawn of a vacant house, hopping a fence that lead to the backyard and alleyway behind it. He ran several feet, before tossing the handgun into someone's backyard, before making it to the end of the alley.

The patrol car came to a screeching halt, as the passenger jumped out giving chase. The police car zoomed down the block, hoping to cut Solomon off as it turned into the alley. The officer inside the car, notices Solomon hopping a fence that lead to someone's backyard. Several feet behind him, is an exhausted officer, breathing out of control. He climbs the fence, in pursuit of Solomon. The police vehicle comes to a complete stop, backing up and zooming around the corner. Solomon trips over something, causing him to stumble several feet, before his body slammed onto the asphalt, leaving him unconscious in the middle of the street. Moments later, the officer on foot, puts his knee into Solomon's back, while cuffing him up. The police car makes it to where the two are at, in the middle of the street, coming to a stop. Officer Milano jumps out of the car highly upset, that he had to chase Solomon down, he hates running.

He snatches Solomon's unconscious body off the street by his arm. "You just got on my bad side, you asshole."

The other officer opens the backdoor of the patrol car, as Milano tosses him into the backseat slamming the door. The activity slowly brings Solo into consciousness.

Officer Milano and his partner doubled back from where the chase began, looking for contraband. Thirty minutes later, they came back with the handgun. Solomon was sent to the Carson Sheriff station, then to Los Padrinos juvenile hall.

October 5, 1987   Monday 7:00 a.m.

EIGHT

"Spencer! Spencer!" yelled the correctional staff, as he banged on the door.

A startled Solomon jumped out of his bed and walked to the door's window, trying to get logically connected. "Was'sup?"

"You have ten minutes, get ready," said the staff.

"Where am I going?"

"To unit N-O," the male staff shot back.

"Alright," said Solomon, becoming a little nervous.

This was his first time at Los Padrinos Juvenile Detention Center. He's preparing himself for what he is about to encounter. He flops down on the bunk and slips on his juvenile issued shoes which are blue Vans. Afterwards, he falls back on the bed exhaling in deep thought. Fifteen minutes later, Solomon's thoughts were interrupted by the knocking on his door.

"Spencer, let's go!"

The door pops open, Solomon steps into the hallway where two other juveniles are standing, looking at Solomon, with frowns on their faces. Solomon nervously nods his head at the two, acknowledging their presence. The two gang bangers become more upset at Solomon's alertness.

"You guys form a single file line, please," ordered the male staff, firmly. They followed his order, with Solomon getting at the end. "Okay, walk into the day room and have a seat. I'm going to grab two more people, then take you guys to your units."

The empty day room is full of plastic chairs. The two juveniles in front of Solomon quickly grabbed a seat, still giving him unpleasant stares. Solomon took a seat several chairs away.

One juvenile got Solomon's attention. "Say loc, where you from?" asked Baby Bone, from Original Front Hood Compton Crips. Baby Bone is five foot-six, high yellow with a stocky built frame and French braids, that comes to his shoulders.

Solomon frowned from his question. "This West Side Piru. Where you from?"

"Front Hood Compton Crip, cuz," Baby Bone responded, upset at Solomon's affiliation.

"This Pocket Hood Compton Crip, cuz," added Lil Blue, who is short and fat, with French braids that stops in the middle of his head, matching his ashy black complexion.

"So what nigga, this Rolling One Thirties," Solomon shot back, flashing a Piru sign with both hands.

"This P.K. cuz," said Baby Bone. P.K. stands for Piru killer, this is a diss to all Pirus.

"Yeah fool, I'm in here for killing your homeboy on Grandee and a hundred and thirty-second, blood," Solomon lied, with a smirk on his face. "Yeah blood, that was me in that black 86' Maxima last month. I domed your homie ol' crab ass nigga."

Not only did Solomon disrespect the two by calling them crabs, a derogatory term used by the bloods. Baby Bone knew he was telling the truth about his homeboy being killed, because he was the other Crip standing on the sidewalk. He saw the whole incident unfold right in front of him. Baby Bone went blank, thinking about it.

Lil Blue looked at Baby Bone confused. "Say loc, that fool killed the homeboy, Midnight, cuz?"

"You talking about that nigga that was walking that red nose pit bull? I smoked Midnight, in broad daylight," Solomon interrupted, chuckling.

"Aw, cuz! Let's rush this fool!" said Lil Blue, jumping out of his seat, with his fist balled up.

Something came over Baby Bone, he jumped out of his seat screaming and crying charging towards Solomon. Lil Blue joined him in the attack. The noise alerted the staff members, in the control booth several feet away. However, they set the whole thing up, already knowing how it was going to unfold. This is how staff members pass their time, watching others get hurt.

Solomon jumped onto his feet and struck Baby Bone with a two piece to the face, causing him to stumble into the plastic chairs that were alongside the wall. Lil Blue caught Solomon on the side of his face, with a wild running punch that dropped him on the floor. Lil Blue followed up with a kick, that struck Solomon in the ribs. Solomon crawled on his hands and knees like a stray dog trying to avoid being hit, by a speeding vehicle. When he got out of striking distance, he jumped onto his feet ready to get active.

"You got me twisted cuz, this Compton Crip fool!" stated Lil Blue, trying to catch his breath while flashing various Compton Crip gang signs with his hands, showing Solomon a lack of respect.

Baby Bone stood onto his feet trying to shake off the dizziness, that had him discombobulated for the moment. "This Front Hood cuz!"

"Fuck both of you crabs blood, this Piru!" responded Solomon, as he rushed Lil Blue

The two went toe to toe, exchanging blows back and forth, seeing who's going to drop first. Baby Bone jumped in, striking Solomon in the back of the head, causing him to stumble. The two Crips rushed Solomon with force swinging and kicking.

"Hey! Stop it! Stop it!" yelled four staff members, as they rushed in the day room to break up the brawl, by grabbing the Crips and pinning them to the ground.

One staff member grabbed Solomon and walked him to the other side of the day room, out of harm's way.

"You crab ass niggas didn't do nothing blood, on Piru!" stated Solomon, whose face was turning red from the blows that he received.

"Ca-rip! Ca-rip! ca-ca-ca-rip!" chanted Lil Blue.

Solomon chuckled, but inside his pride was hurt that the two Crips got out on him. "Yeah, y'all got that blood. This still Piru fool!"

All the staff members grew smirks on their faces as they held onto the angry gang bangers. Moments later, each affiliate went to their separate housing units. Solomon was placed in unit N-O, on the O-wing. The unit was filled with gang members from both sides of the color barrier. Since the incident with Lil Blue and Baby Bone, Solomon now has a personal grudge with all Crips from Compton. Whenever he spots one no matter where: school, church, court, or whenever a new one arrives in the unit, he's attacking them on the spot. Solomon's reputation quickly grew inside Los Padrinos, amongst the staff and gang bangers alike, because of his don't give a fuck attitude, of going back and forth to the hole which is known as the Box.

After being shuttled back and forth to court for thirty days. Solomon was given a track three camp program, which is a maximum term of 9-12 months at Camp Gonzales, in Malibu California. The sentence was stiff being that this was his first time ever in trouble. But everyone knew, that if you had to appear in front of Judge Fletcher in Long Beach, your ass is pretty much through. He has a hard-on for gang members especially Crips, being that his daughter was gang raped and his son was robbed and murdered by them. A week later, Solomon was shipped to Sylmar Juvenile Hall.

*****

Since Solomon's absence, Mrs. Milano has been having an attitude with students, especially with Tina-ru; who constantly reminds her that Solomon is her man. She even went as far as to tell her about the night that they had sex, causing Mrs. Milano's blood to boil. Every time Mrs. Milano would inquire about Solomon's whereabouts, Tina-ru would spin her with lies, saying that he transferred to another school and moved to another city. On several occasions after class, Mrs. Milano took it upon herself to cruise through his neighborhood searching for him, only to come up empty handed each time. It finally dawned on Mrs. Milano, there is only one place that he could be. Mrs. Milano did her investigation.

*****

It's been twenty-four hours since Solomon has been inside the box, at Sylmar. His nap was interrupted by the banging of his door.

"Spencer wake-up, you're about to go to your unit," said the staff member as he walked away.

"Alright," responded Solomon, who quickly jumped out of bed looking out the door's window. Solomon placed his lips on the door's crack. "Hey, do you know what unit I'm going too?"

"I'm not sure, you'll find out in the day room," responded the staff, from a distance.

Another juvenile in the door's window across the hall from Solomon, gets his attention. This is Baby Spank, from Eighty-Seven Street, Gangster Crip gang in Los Angeles. Baby Spank is a notorious cell soldier and Thorazine patient, that lives inside the box. "Say homie, where you from?"

"I'm from West Side, Piru," Solomon answered nonchalantly.

"This Eight Seven Gangster Crip, cuz!" screamed Baby Spank, from the top of his lungs, while flashing gang signs in the window at Solomon.

"Fuck you blood. I'm not gonna feed into your little game, fool," Solomon replied in a low tone, as he flipped him the bird through the door's window, before flopping down back onto his bunk.

Baby Spank continued to scream disrespectful slurs at Solomon through the door. Another cell solider got on the door and began heckling Baby Spank. The two went at it verbally, until several staff members came on the range demanding silence. After making several threats to the two juveniles' safety, their demand was met.

"Spencer let's go," said the staff, as he unlocked Solomon's door. Solomon stepped out into the middle of the hallway. "Place your hands behind your back and follow me please."

As Solomon walked down the corridor towards the day room, he begins to flashback the day room incident at Los Padrinos. He mentally psyched himself up by thinking of his favorite rap song; 'Nobody beats the biz,' by Biz Markie. This song gets him ready for whatever.

As Solomon reaches the door to the day room his heart beats uncontrollably, but slows down when he notices that it's empty. He flops down into a plastic chair and begin tapping his fingers from both hands on his knees out of nervousness.

Five minutes later, four male juveniles walked into the day room with frowns on their faces. Solomon eyed all of them trying to put a name to their faces as they all took a seat in the plastic chairs. Solomon twisted his two braided ponytails into one, preparing for the worse.

"Hey, homie, where y'all from?" Solomon asked, talking to all the potential rival gang bangers.

One juvenile leaped out of his chair onto his feet standing six feet even, with an oily black skin complexion, sporting a short nappy afro probably weighing about one hundred and fifty pounds soaking wet. "This two P's and a B. Pacoima Piru Blood, what's happening?" he asked, flashing Piru signs with both hands.

"Oh, what's up Piru?" Solomon asked becoming excited, that another blood was amongst him. "Who is them other fools?"

The Pacoima Piru hunched his shoulders. "I don't know where these fools are from." he replied in a low tone, while looking at the three. "Say, homie, where y'all fools from?"

A short fat pudgy built high yellow complexion juvenile with a dried-out jheri-curl stood onto his feet, flashing a gang sign as he spoke. "This West Side Pasadena Denver Lanes, blood."

The other two juveniles were looking away, as if they were trying to avoid representing their affiliation.

"Y'all two must be some crabs," asked the Pacoima Piru.

One caramel complexion juvenile, standing at five-foot nine and a hundred and seventy pounds, stood onto his feet with both fist balled up. It's mandatory that gang members let their affiliation be known, under any circumstances. "Nawh, cuz, I'mma Crip. I'm from Du- Roc."

"Fuck dirt rock blood, this Lane," stated the Pasadena Denver Lane. Dirt rock is a disrespectful term towards Du-roc Crips.

"Fuck ding-a-lings cuz, this Du-roc," replied the Du-roc Crip, defending his hood. Ding-a-ling is a disrespectful term towards Denver Lanes.

"Hey! Sit y'all asses down!" yelled one muscular black staff member, walking into the day room, with an extra small shirt trying to intimidate the juveniles. "I leave you muthafucka alone for one minute and here y'all go with the bullshit! All of you guys better learn how to get along up here in Sylmar, because we'll beat y'all asses."

This juvenile hall is in San Fernando Valley and eighty percent of its occupants are local gangs, such as Pacoima Pirus, Pacoima Thirteen, Pasadena Denver Lanes, Pasadena Squigley Lanes, Pasadena Raymond Crips, Altadena Block Crips, Pomona 456, Pomona 357's, The Island, Pomona Thirteen and Ghost Town Crips.

Another black male staff, with salt and pepper hair walks into the day room. "Alright gentlemen, line up so you can go to your designated housing units. Form two lines and place your hands behind your back." The juveniles followed his order, with Solomon heading the line.

"Alright, I'm giving you guys a fair warning. Do not speak to anyone while we're walking and no gang signs. If I catch you doing any of the two, your ass is out," warned the staff, with the extra small shirt. He opened the doors unit and stepped out. "Alright, let's go." Solomon was the first one to step out of the door. He squinted his eyes, from the bright seventy-five-degree sunlight, that shined over the facility. Sylmar looks more like a college campus, compared to Los Padrinos or Central juvenile hall in Downtown L.A. However, this facility is new only being in existence for ten years. Juveniles with good behaviors, can go swimming in the institution's pool, that sits in the center of the facility, surrounded by a well-manicured lawn. The units are labeled from A-Z, in alphabetical order and the group of juveniles must stop at each unit, picking up and dropping off juveniles as they make their rounds twice a day, in the morning and noon.

The four juveniles put it on thick, walking extra hard as they passed each unit, knowing that they're being looked at through the windows of each unit. They reach unit E-F stopping at the front door.

"When I call your name, step out of the line and wait in front of the unit's door," said the male staff with the extra small shirt. "Spencer and Townsend."

Solomon and the other juvenile from Pacoima Piru stepped out the line and waited by the door. Within seconds, a staff member opened the door and stepped out, acknowledging the other staff with the extra small shirt that he has the two new arrivals. He nodded his head and continued walking with the juveniles throughout the institution.

"Step inside gentlemen," demanded the short stocky built, African male staff. He stepped in front of Solomon, inches from his face mad dogging him. "I don't like you fool, where you from?"

Solomon frowned back at the staff. "I'm from West Side Piru Blood," Solomon stated, not breaking eye contact with the staff.

The staff continued looking at Solomon in the eyes, not saying a word, then looked him up and down sizing Solomon up. "Why are your finger nails so long, are you gay?"

"Nawh is you?" Solomon shot back.

"I'mma put you on the range with all the Crips," said the short stocky staff.

Solomon hunched his shoulders. "I don't give a fuck what you do blood. This Piru."

The short stocky staff has a little man's complex. This is his way of feeling secure bluffing and intimidating juveniles. However, he sees Solomon wasn't going for it, so he backed off him. He walked over to the Pacoima Piru and repeated the same process by staring him in the eyes. "Where you from fool?"

"This two P's and a B blood. Pacoima Piru," He responded, flashing gang signs in both hands in the shape of a 'P'.

The staff member chuckled. "Is that right? What they call you?"

"Crab Crusher," he shot back.

"Oh, is that right? I'mma put you on the range with some Crips. I wanna see how tuff you are," responded the staff.

"Yeah, you gonna see," Crab Crusher, responded

Both of y'all take a seat over there in those plastic chairs. Solomon and Crab Crusher does so.

Solomon chuckled." Hey Piru, I like your name blood."

Crab Crusher smiled. "What they call you homie?"

"Solo," Solomon responded, extending his hand out to him. They both do the Piru handshake.

"Do you know where they're gonna send you?" asked Crab Crusher.

"Well, they said I'm going to a long-term lock down camp. But I don't see how, when this is my first time ever doing a camp program," Solomon responded.

"Oh, there ain't but two places they're gonna send you.

Camp Rocky in San Dimas or Camp Gonzales, in Malibu," explained Crab Crusher. "Either way, you're gonna be straight. It's a gang of homies in Camp Gonzales. I got five homies from my hood up there alone. They shooting me to either Camp Paige or Camp Louis Roth. Those are fire camps."

"Oh, yeah?" asked Solomon, out of curiosity.

"Yeah, I'mma go up there for a minute and come back on super swole," responded Crab Crusher, poking his chest out making his chest muscles jump on both sides through his sweat shirt. They both burst out into laughter from his shenanigans, he's nothing but skin and bones.

"Where ever I go, I'm gonna represent Piru to the fullest," Solomon stated, becoming excited.

"Blood, that's mando (mandatory) homie," Crab Crusher shot back.

The two carry on in conversation for about an hour uninterrupted, before the short stocky staff member appears back into the day room. "Alright gentlemen, you guys line up. We're going to pick up the rest of the guys from school," stated the stocky staff member.

The two does so. The staff opens the door and the three walks to the school area picking up juveniles from each class. By the time they return to the unit, there are thirty juveniles in total. All the adolescents took a seat in the plastic chairs.

"Orderlies set up the day room for lunch," stated the short stocky, staff member as he exited the day room.

Three juveniles get up from the plastic chairs and started setting up the day room for lunch, by pulling out the tables that folds into the walls. Within twenty minutes the day room was set up for lunch. Everyone took a seat at the tables and began devouring the recommended portion. The short stocky staff left the day room and sat in the glass booth, that oversees the day room. He knew that once his presence was away from the day room, someone was going to approach Solomon and Crab Crusher inquiring about their gang affiliation.

The only noise that can be heard is the smacking of each individual eating. The prisoners are not allowed to talk while eating their meals.

One grotesque looking individual sitting across from Solomon, dark skinned with a short nappy afro packed with lint and dirt, stares at him with a frown on his face as he eats. Solomon makes eye contact with him then smirks from his theatrics.

"Say homie, where you from?" asked the juvenile in front of him in a low tone.

"West Side Piru," responded Solomon, staring the potential enemy in the eyes. "Where you from?"

"Altadena Block Crip, A-B-C they call me Ugly Cuz," responded Ugly Cuz.

Solomon became somewhat offended. He only asked him where he was from not his name. "This West Side Pi-mutha-fucking-Ru, Rolling One Thirties. I'm Solo blood."

"So, what," Ugly Cuz, shot back.

96

"Fuck you blood," Solomon replied getting loud.

"Don't get loud fool, you trying to check in the hole cuz? We can take it in the bathroom after lunch nigga," explained Ugly Cuz.

Solomon caught himself and lowered his tone. "I ain't no check in fool. After lunch then blood."

"Then after you get down with my homeboy me and you gonna get down blood," interrupted Crab Crusher, in a low tone showing Piru love.

"Where you from?" asked Ugly Cuz, with a frown on his face.

"Two P's and a Bee, Pacoima Piru Blood. Big Crab Crusher," replied Crab Crusher, in a firm tone staring at Ugly Cuz.

All the Crips in the day room became offended, from him stating his name. They all stared at him as they ate their food but remained silent. Five minutes later, the staff member saw that everyone was finished with their meal, so he walked back into the day room. He was also aware of the fight invitation between Ugly Cuz, Solomon and Crab Crusher, courtesy of the day room's speaker that can be heard in the staff's office. The short stocky staff member admired the two Pirus. He wished that he had balls like them. But they had many more tests to pass.

"Alright, everyone go to your cells, except for Spencer and Townsend, who has not been assigned to a cell yet" stated the short stocky staff member. "Oh and my orderlies, clean this mess up please."

All the juveniles walked away grilling Solomon and Crab Crusher, except for the Hispanics and several Bloods, that walked by flashing Blood signs at the two, letting them know that it ain't all Crips in the unit. Solomon and Crab Crusher acknowledged the Bloods, by flashing gang signs back at them. Solomon and Crab Crusher sat in the row of plastic chairs, so that the orderlies could clean the area. Twenty minutes later, they were assigned cells. Crab Crusher is in the front part of the range and Solomon is way in the back.

Solomon flopped down onto his bunk in deep contemplation. The cells in this facility are spacious, especially being that it's a single man room. The view is also much better than Los Padrinos and Central put together. At those facilities the only view from your window is a twenty-foot wall. Here at Sylmar, the facility was built right next to the freeway and from Solomon's cell, you can see the on-ramp. Everyone that's housed in that cell count the vehicles as they pass, to pass their time. However, this institution doesn't play oldies but goodies like Central or Los Padrinos. Over there a juvenile could lie in his bunk and enjoy groups like: The Stylistics, Delfonics, Temprees, Harold Melvin and the Bluenotes, War, L.T.D., Brass Construction, The O'jays, Rolls Royce, Bloodstone and Cameo. Solomon wasn't tripping off that, he had a jukebox inside his head. He fell asleep thinking about his mother, wondering what she was doing.

An hour later, Solomon's nap was interrupted by the banging on his door. He jumped out of the bed startled, heart pounding out of control.

"Hey Spencer, put your shoes and shit on. Somebody is here from the probation department they want to talk to you," said the short stocky staff member.

"Alright, give me a second," said Solomon, as he stood up and walked over to the sink to splash water on his face. He looked at himself in the chrome apparatus that hung on the wall, replacing a glass mirror, wiping his face several times as he becomes connected to what is going on. He quickly placed his shoes on and walked up to the door's window, where the stocky one was waiting.

"Alright, I'm ready."

The short stocky one yelled down the hallway. "I got one coming down!"

"Alright, let's do it!" responded a male voice from a distance.

The short stocky staff member opened the door, to let Solomon out. They walked down the range, until they reached a closet size room, that sits behind the control booth. Inside, was an African American woman, in her mid-forties, heavy set and wearing a pair of throwback eyeglasses, similar to Shirley Chisolm's. She looks up at Solomon smiling, then motions for him to come inside.

Solomon does so and takes a seat in the plastic chair, on the opposite side of her desk. The short stocky staff member closes the door, to give the two some privacy.

"How, you doing Mr. Spencer? My name is Ms. Spencer," she stated, flashing her butter yellow teeth while sticking her hand out to Solomon.

Solomon shook her hand. "How you doing Ms. Spencer? What a coincidence, we might be relatives huh?"

"May-bee," she responded chuckling, as she let go of his hand to arrange the papers inside the folder that sits in front of her. "Well Mr. Spencer, how are they treating you here in Sylmar?"

Solomon tilted his head to the right, poking out his lips. "It's cool, I mean, I can't complain. Jail is jail."

"Well, I have some good news and maybe some bad news. Which one do you want to hear first?" asked Ms. Spencer.

Solomon chuckled. "Let me hear the good news, first."

"Alright well, originally, you were sent to a long-term lock down camp. We had you in route to Camp Rocky in San Dimas, someone in a higher place had some say-so and now you're being sent to Camp 15. I guess this person, had your record reviewed and got you shipped there," explained Ms. Spencer.

"Who did that?"

"Your guess is just a good as mine. But whoever pulled those strings looked out for you. Camp 15 is a much better facility that fights brush fires and it's an open camp.

Solomon sat in silence for a moment nodding in agreement. "So, what's the bad news?"

"The bad news is. You're still a track three program and a track three is a nine to twelve-month program, with nine months being the lease and a year being the maximum," responded Ms. Spencer, with a sad look on her face.

Solomon smiled, "It's all good, at least I can learn about fires and get in shape."

"That's right! See with your good attitude, they should let you out in nine months," said Ms. Spencer, smiling. "I wish there were more young men who thought like you. Your mother did a great job of raising you, I bet she is proud of you."

Solomon's smile was cut short from the thought of his mother and Ms. Spencer's knowledge of Chinadoll. "Yeah I wish she was. I think you're more proud of me than she is."

"I don't mean to be in your business, but are you and your mother having communication problems?"

Solomon smiled from Ms. Spencer's way of probing. "No, I don't mind. But yes, my mother and I have been having communication problems all our life. I'm a pariah in her eyes."

Ms. Spencer was taken aback from his statement, nodding her head in agreement. "How is your relationship with the rest of your family?"

"Well, I don't know my father cause I'm a trick baby or love child, which ever term you wanna use. My grandmother is real sweet and we get along great. My sisters, I love them too but I'm tired of being their sex slave. My brothers, I'm cool with them, but my mother uses them as puppets and we fight on call, at my mother's command. And all of this happens to me, because her husband used to rent her out to my father and when she came up pregnant her husband thought that they were having another child. But when I was born and he realized that I wasn't his, he divorced her, then he was murdered by rival gang members with the assistance of the Carson Sheriff. So psychologically, she's fucked up in the head, to think that I had something to do with their prostitution scam going wrong. I didn't do nothing but what I was supposed to do, be born and live," explained Solomon, after looking at Ms. Spencer's face smiling.

Ms. Spencer sat in silence stunned. So underneath all that beauty, and brains is a sick little son-of-a-bitch ready to explode! With all of that shit that he's going through, he's just a disaster waiting to happen! Ms. Spencer thought to herself. After collecting her thoughts, she placed her papers back into her folder, while flashing a warm smile at Solomon.

"Well Mr. Spencer, on that note it's time for us to close. Bye."

Solomon chuckled, he is used to people responding the way that she did. "I hope I didn't scare you off"

"Oh, no, no, no, I'm used to hearing those type of stories trust me, I've heard worse," replied a lying Ms. Spencer. Let me get away from this sicko before he lashes out at me. "Okay he's finished, bring me the next one!" She said out loud, to the short stocky staff member. He walked in and removed Solomon from the office and placed him back into his cell.

Solomon laid back on his bunk, with his arms in the back of his head, smiling from the news of going to a fire camp. He visualized himself on swole, what is known as the Cali built; muscles everywhere on top and from waist down, skinny as hell. His thoughts quickly switched over to Mrs. Milano. He couldn't wait until he turned eighteen, to get inside those panties. He imagined himself hitting her doggy style, while choking her from behind, with a red bandana wrapped around his head, Aunt Jemima style. He jumped out of bed, peeking out of his doors window, making sure no one was in the hallway. He then walked over to the toilet, snatching his pants and underwear down to his ankles, then began stroking his manhood quickly, while thinking about his school teacher. Solomon had trouble reaching a climax, maybe because he was stroking his dick dry, almost starting a fire. He knew he didn't have any lubrication inside the cell, so he tried another method. He cupped the tip of his penis, spitting on it, then began stroking it vigorously, until he felt a climax coming from his toes and ass cheeks. Moments later, he felt electricity throughout his whole body, until he ejaculated, shooting the semen onto the wall, milking his hose, of every drop. Solomon felt great, he pulled his pants back up, then fell backwards onto his bunk and took a nap.

November 15, 1987   Monday 9:00 a.m.

NINE

Solomon and Crab Crusher waited in the transportation room with two other juveniles. A Mexican and an Asian.

"Blood, what's the first thing you're gonna do when we get to Camp 15?" asked Crab Crusher, pacing back and forth inside the room's minimal space.

Solomon thought for a moment, rubbing his chin. "I don't know, probably get something to eat. I heard they eat really good up there."

"Hell, yeah, steaks and shit," interrupted Little Shadow, from Barrio thirteen, a Hispanic gang in Los Angeles. "I got a homeboy who just came home from that camp."

"Oh, yeah?" asked Solomon. "Where they sending you to?"

"Camp Carl Holton," answered Lil Shadow.

"Oh, okay," Solomon replied. He made eye contact with the Asian kid. "Where are, they sending you to homie?"

"I'm going to Carl Holton," replied the Asian.

"Right, Right," Solomon responded.

Their conversation was cut short, by a forty-year-old white female staff member, opening the door to the room they're waiting in. "When I call your name, come and get your property and put your clothes on, so we can drive you guys to your facilities. The faster you guys get dressed, the sooner we can leave. Townsend, Spencer, Diaz and Lee. Come grab your shit and get dressed."

The white female slid their property into the room with her foot, then quickly closed the door shut.

Each juvenile grabbed their bags, opening them up like they were Christmas presents. They quickly put on the clothes that they were arrested in.

Everyone looked at each other's gear, seeing who had on the best. But for some reason, everyone's attention was on Solomon, who had on burgundy clothing from head to toe.

"Damn homeboy, they must have caught you on the block huh?" asked Crab Crusher. "You banged out dog."

Solomon smiled, looking down at his burgundy high top Chuck Taylors and matching khaki shirt and pants. "Nawh, I'm like this every day blood."

"Hey ese, where you from?" asked Lil Shadow, who is dressed in an all brown khaki suit and black Romeos (shoes) polished up.

"I'm from West Side Piru, Rolling One Thirties," Solomon stated, firmly.

"Oh okay, I'm from B-13, Holmes," responded Lil Shadow, giving Solomon some dap. Their neighborhoods are in the same vicinity.

"Right, Right," Solomon replied, then he looked over at crab Crusher. "Shit, if I was an enemy coming to shoot some Pirus, I would shoot you because you look like a homie."

"Who me? Hell nawh," said Crab Crusher, answering his own question, looking down at his attire. "I look more like a crab than anything. If I didn't have on this Pirate cap you couldn't tell. I got on black Chuck Taylors and a black khaki suit. I look nothing like you blood."

The four juveniles burst into laughter from his statement. Then they all keyed in on the Asian kid, who is dressed in a pair of checkerboard Vans, a pair of black tight fitting Levi jeans and a dingy t-shirt.

"What are you homie, a skateboarder?" asked Solomon.

The Asian kid smiled. "Yep, how did you know? From the way I'm dressed?"

"Most definitely," Solomon replied laughing.

The four hoodlums became silent, as the door of the room flew open. The white female ordered the four out of the room and directed them to the van, so that they can be transported to their facilities. The white female was joined by a tall Nigerian male, to assist her in transporting the group.

"Place your seat belts on guys thank-you," ordered the white female as she placed hers on, then started up the van.

"Can we hear some 1580 KDAY please, asked Solomon. This is a popular a.m. radio station, that plays rap and R&B music all day.

The white female looked at Solomon through the van's rear view mirror frowning.

She can't stand black music. But if it would keep the four juveniles silent during the ride, then she is all for it. "Does everyone agree to listen to the same station?"

The four thugs looked at each other nodding in approval.

"Yes ma'am," Solomon replied, politely. He knew the white female was a miserable bitch, but knew how to use the power of words by stroking her with politeness. She switched the station to 1580 KDAY; Solomon smiled. "Thank-you, ma'am."

"You're welcome," responded the white female in a low tone.

The group nodded their heads to the song 'Supersonic' by J.J. Fad, especially little Shadow. Mexicans love that song.

The white female sped out of the detention bureau's parking lot, causing everyone to brace themselves. She quickly jumped onto the freeway in route to Camp Carl Holton. She planned on getting to both camps in half the time that it usually takes.

The four-remained silent, as they listened to songs from: Boogie Down Productions, Biz Markie, L.L. Cool J, Easy-E, World Class Wreckin Crew, Egyptian Lover, Ice-T, Eric B & Rakim, The L.A. Dream Team, Public Enemy, Roxanne Shante, Big Daddy Kane and Bobby Jimmy and the Critters. Before they knew it, the van was speeding up the driveway that lead to the entrance of Camp Holton. The white female turned down the radio as she pulled up to the speaker box, that opens the facilities gate. After identifying her presence, the gate opened and she drove onto the camp grounds parking by the office.

"Alright, Diaz and Lee this is you guy's stop," said the white female, turning off the van, unbuckling her seat belt and exiting the vehicle. She walked around to the sliding side door to let them out.

The two unbuckled their seat belts, said their goodbyes and departed. Solomon and Crab Crusher looked on as the two walked into the camps office.

"You guys are going to a much better camp than this one. This camp is for more hardcore juveniles. You guys must be locked up for purse snatching; or grand theft auto, cause the camp you guys are going to is open and you can walk away from that facility, at any given time," stated the tall Nigerian, with a heavy accent, looking over his left shoulder at the two Pirus.

The two Pirus looked at the Nigerian staff with smirks on their faces. Both are young, but secure with their status as gang members, so they didn't feed into his statement. The foolish staff member saw that he couldn't get them to bite, so he turned back around and kept his mouth shut. Five minutes later, the white female returned to the van and sped off the camp grounds in route to Camp Louis Roth, which is known as Camp 15. Since the juveniles gave the white female no problems, she turned the radio back on so that Solomon and Crab Crusher can remain on quiet, until they reach their camp.

After enjoying up beat songs from: Ready for the World, Lisa-Lisa and the Cult Jam, Alexander O'Neal, Cherelle, Levert, Cameo, New Edition, and Orange Juice Jones; the van sped down Big Tujunga Canyon road, only feet away from Camp 15.

The white female staff turned off the radio. "Alright you guys, we're about to pull up to your facility. I wanna thank you guys for being mature, throughout this journey. Usually, when I take this trip, I have to verbally abuse individuals because of their immaturity. But once again, I wanna thank you guys for being respectful."

"No problem, that's how the Pirus do it. We give respect, but demand it in return," Solomon responded.

"Same here," the white female answered.

The van slowed down, as it made its way up the ramp. Solomon and Crab Crusher glued their faces on the van's window, in awe at what they saw. Camp 15, has three units in a tandem: an outhouse, a small kitchen, a chapel, a school house and a small visiting area. This camp is small, only housing a hundred juveniles and that's at its maximum occupancy. The van parked in front of the office; Solomon and Crab Crusher unbuckled their seat belts preparing to make their departure.

The Nigerian looked over his shoulder at the two Pirus. "Hey, you guys take it easy."

"Alright," the two said in unison, as they scooted towards the van's, sliding door.

The white female opened the side sliding door of the van, letting the two out. "Welcome home guys."

Both Pirus slowly climbed out of the van, squinting their eyes from the brightness of the sun. Although it was November, the temperature was still somewhere in the mid-sixties. A few inmates were cleaning the camp grounds; once they noticed the new booties, they gave them hard stares. The Pirus returned the stares, as they strolled up the stairs that led them to the main office. They were met at the door by a short Mexican man, in his early thirties by the name of Mr. Rodriquez. In the face, Mr. Rodriquez looked just like the low-rider magazine logo, thick black hair on his head, dark shades and a thick black broom looking mustache.

"Come inside guys and take a seat on the leather couch inside the office," said Mr. Rodriquez, who grabbed two brown looking files out of the white female's hands. "Alright ma'am, we got it from here. Thank you."

"Alright, take care," she responded, jumping back in the van speeding off.

Mr. Rodriquez walked into the office where the two Pirus were sitting and sat at the desk in front of them, making eye contact with the two sizing them up. "Where are you guys from?" "Pacoima," responded Crab Crusher, smiling.

"Compton," Solomon added proudly.

"You guys gang bang?" asked Mr. Rodriquez.

"Yeah, I'm from Piru," answered Crab Crusher.

"You too," Mr. Rodriquez asked Solomon.

"Yeah, I'm from West Side Piru," Solomon stated.

Mr. Rodriquez responded, by nodding his head at the two in deep thought. "You know, I was checking you guys out when y'all stepped off the van. You guys were looking for trouble, by the way y'all was mad-dogging everybody on your way up to the office." Solomon and Crab Crusher looked at each other out of confusion.

"We have approximately ninety-five inmates here, twenty of them are Crips and there are about thirty Bloods here, including you two. The other forty-five, are a mixture of Surenos and non-affiliations," explained Mr. Rodriquez, twirling his thumbs. "And let me say this, this is a work camp; as of now, everyone is either out working forestry or at the fire station in Pasadena, rolling up fire hoses. So, if you guys don't wanna work, we can send you to Camp Rocky or Gonzalez. Also, every day you must be well groomed. I'm talking about your fingernails must be clipped, your face must be smooth, no stubble, shirt tucked in, pants pulled up, boots polished and you have to exercise every morning, Monday thru Friday, before you have breakfast."

"Damn blood." Responded Crab Crusher.

"Oh yeah, I forgot, that hair has to come off," added Mr. Rodriquez, looking directly at Solomon. Crab Crusher hair is nowhere as long as Solomon's, so he wasn't sweating the hair thing.

"I ain't tripping, it'll grow back," responded Solomon, he knew that Mr. Rodriquez was waiting for him to say something negative but he remained cool.

"Also, every day you guys are graded on your daily conduct and at the end of every week, if you guys don't have a certain amount of points, you can't go to the movies and enjoy popcorn while you're watching the movie," Mr. Rodriquez pointed out with a smirk on his face.

"How many points are required at the end of every week?" Solomon asked out of curiosity.

"Four hundred and if you're doing really good and stay in the top ten for a couple of weeks, you get to go with Ms. Martinez," explained Mr. Rodriquez.

"Go with Ms. Martinez where?" asked Crab Crusher.

"Every month, Ms. Martinez takes ten people of her choice, that's in the top twenty merit ladder, to a play or a movie theater on the streets. "Is she young and pretty," Solomon asked smiling.

"Nawh, she's an old hag. She's gonna be working your unit tonight, so you'll get a chance to see her. Plus, she likes it when you guys jerk off to her while listening to the Isley Brothers," responded Mr. Rodriquez.

The Pirus looked at each other out of disbelief of Mr. Rodriquez's statement. However, it was music to the young pervert's ears.

"I'm liking this camp already," stated Solomon with a smile on his face.

"Well, we'll see how much you'll like it after you hike Kill 'em Quick," said Mr. Rodriquez.

"Kill 'em Quick? What's that?" asked Crab Crusher.

"That huge mountain that's about a half a mile away. Everyone must hike Kill 'em Quick, even the staff members. If you can make it to the top under thirty minutes, that means that you're in shape," Mr. Rodriquez responded.

"Aw, that ain't shit," Crab Crusher responded.

"I already see right now, you're gonna get a lot of downgrades for cursing," said Mr. Rodriquez. "You're gonna be polishing boots."

"Polishing boots?" asked a confused Crab Crusher. "That's what you have to do when you can't go to the movies?"

"That and make up your bed, making sure it has hospital corners. But the good part, you can write all the letters you want," explained Mr. Rodriquez smiling. "Well guys, the nurse needs to see you. When you finish with her, you can go to your designated dorms. One of your homeboys will give you a tour of the place."

An African American woman in her late thirties steps into the office. "Spencer and Townsend come with me please."

The two jumped up and followed the nurse into her office. "Have a seat please. My name is Ms. Crutchfield, if you guys have any medical problems notify me okay?"

"Okay," responded Crab Crusher.

"Yes ma'am?" said Solomon in a singing tone.

Ms. Crutchfield began to blush profusely, as she felt Solomon eye fucking her. She knew that she had it going on physically and the compliments from all the young horny juveniles in the facility, is what motivated her to keep her 38-24-38 physique nice and firm. Five days a week, she comes to work sporting an all-white snug fitting nurses outfit, that exposes her legs and just enough cleavage, to run a juvenile imagination wild. But on the flip side, Ms. Crutchfield was known around the camp as a bitch. Her actions were obvious, she had no love for you if you weren't black; she couldn't stand Mexicans or whites and if they needed medical attention, they got the basics. Plus, if any of them has the balls to make a cat call or wondering eyes towards her, their asses are going to the hole; no exceptions. What pissed her off about the blacks, is that they'll make a pass at her, but wouldn't follow through with it. She's waiting for that one juvenile with nuts, to pull his dick out and stroke it while she watches or bend her over a chair, for a quickie. Verbally, she can't tell them to do it, because it'll kill her fantasy and possibly cost her job. But as far as her actions go, the writing was on the wall. She looked at Solomon with lust in her eyes. "What nationality are you?"

"Black, White and Asian," Solomon responded.

"Mmmmph, mmph, mmph," moaned Ms. Crutchfield, as she grabbed one of his braids rubbing it in-between her fingers. "It's a shame, you know they're gonna cut all of your hair off."

"Yeah, I heard. I ain't tripping though," Solomon lied, rolling his eyes at the thought.

Damn! This old bitch is on fire! Crab Crusher thought to himself, as he watched the nurse look at Solomon, as if she was ready to jump his bones. I wish she was on me like that, damn!

Ms. Crutchfield stood over Solomon. "Do you have any questions?"

Solomon thought for a moment. "Nawh, I'm good."

"What about you?" she asked, looking over at Crab Crusher.

Yeah bitch! Come over here and rub my hair and shit. Crab Crusher screamed in thought. "No ma'am, I'm good."

"Alright, remember what I told you guys. If you need anything, just come up and see me," said Ms. Crutchfield, dropping a hint at the two Pirus indirectly.

Solomon caught on. "Anything?" asked Solomon, in a low seductive tone making eye contact with the nurse.

"I said anything, didn't I?" she responded, hoping that Solomon had enough brains to figure out what she was saying figuratively and enough balls to follow up literally.

"So, if I want something and I can't get it until I go home; I could come holler at you and you'll make sure that I get taken care of, right?" Solomon asked bluntly, making sure that they were on the same page.

Ms. Crutchfield formed a devilish smirk onto her face, while winking her right eye at him. "There you go."

"Alright, I'mma take you up on that offer," Solomon shot back in a low tone. "I hope you're not pulling my leg."

"Hmmph, that's what they all say, but no one ever follows up," said Ms. Crutchfield, becoming disappointed.

"Nawh, I think you got me confused with these other cats. I'mma Piru," Solomon stated proudly.

Ms. Crutchfield rolled her eyes, chuckling at Solomon's foolish statement. "Well, I hope I don't have you confused with the other fifteen Pirus out there on the compound."

Solomon stood up and slowly exited the office. Crab crusher followed behind. "Alright I'mma holler at you later."

Ms. Crutchfield folded her arms across her chest responding nonchalantly. "Alright, Mr. Piru."

The two walked into the office where Mr. Rodriquez is sitting, thumbing through a reader's digest magazine. He looks up and notices the two. "Are you guys squared away?"

"Yeah," the two said in unison.

"Alright, let's roll out," suggested Mr. Rodriquez, as he stood up from his desk and walked out of the office. The two Pirus followed behind.

As the three walked across the compound, Mr. Rodriquez pointed out the out of bounds areas, warning them to respect the huge red line. If not, they were going to the hole for seven days. After pointing out several other areas of the jail, they finally reached C-dorm and walked inside.

Solomon and Crab Crusher looked throughout the unit in awe. On one side of the unit, there were over twenty bunk beds in a row, with metal lockers in between them. On the other side of the unit, were a row of twenty single twin size beds, with the same lockers in between them. In the center of the unit, was a fat white man sitting at a huge metal desk, with a cassette stereo playing 'Human Nature,' by Michael Jackson. This is Mr. Grebel, One of the staffs here at Camp 15.

"Alright, we have two new contestants here at Camp Louis Roth. Let's see how long they last," Mr. Grebel announced to the other juveniles jokingly. The juveniles chuckled as they sat on their bunk beds with their hands on their knees, in an upright military fashion.

What the fuck have I got myself into? Solomon thought to himself.

The three reach the desk where Mr. Grebel is sitting. "Alright, Mr. Rodriquez, I got it from here thank-you."

"Alright Mr. Grebel, they all yours," responded Mr. Rodriquez as he walked off. After taking several steps, Mr. Rodriquez turned back around. "Hey, I forgot to tell you. You gotta keep your eyes on them two, they're both Pirus. One is from Compton and the other one is from Pacoima."

All the juveniles inside the dorm looked at the two; some were smiling while the others were frowning.

"Oh yeah, Pirus huh? Well, we're all in the same gang here. We all represent Camp 15," explained Mr. Grebel. He then became animated, by flashing various gang signs with both hands. "What's up fool? This Camp Louis Roth. Where y'all from?"

Solomon and Crab Crusher looked at each other chuckling from Mr. Grebel foolishness.

"I'm joking. How you guys doing? I'm Mr. Grebel," Mr. Grebel introduced himself, by shaking both of their hands. "Which one of you guys are Townsend?"

"Me," responded Crab Crusher raising his hand.

"Alright Townsend, you're on my caseload. Do you need a phone call?"

"Um yeah, yes sir," Crab Crusher shot back.

"Alright, when my relief shows up I'll give you one. In the meantime, you guys can hang out at the end of the unit, in those

117

plastic chairs, until we assign you a bunk. You guys can talk, but keep it on low chatter. The rest of the dorm is on quiet," ordered Mr. Grebel, lacing his fingers in-between each other resting them on his huge stomach, enjoying the sounds of Michael Jackson.

The two Pirus strolled off looking at the other juveniles with smirks on their faces, flaunting their privilege to talk, while they sit on their bunks looking stupid. The two flop down in the plastic chairs.

"What do you think so far? You think we're gonna last? This shit is a real boot camp blood on Piru," said Crab Crusher in a low tone.

"I don't know blood, this shit is nuts. Look at these fools sitting on their beds, like they're in the military or something," Solomon shot back, in a whispering tone. The two Pirus looked throughout the dorm snickering.

They make eye contact with an average height, brown skinned, muscular built juvenile, with waves in his hair. Once he sees that he has their attention, he secretly form both of his hands that's on his knees, into "P" signs, letting them know that he's a Piru. This is Papoose from Luders Park Pirus in Compton.

Both Solomon and Crab Crusher looked over at Mr. Grebel, who was nodding and responded back to Papoose by flashing Piru signs. Papoose smiled from the love.

Out of nowhere a loud bell can be heard ringing. Mr. Grebel jumped out of his chair startled. "Alright gentlemen, it's chow time. At ease, get ready for lunch."

All the juveniles let out a sigh of relief. Papoose walked over to Solomon and Crab Crusher, and introduced himself. He then briefed them of the camp's rules and regulations, then pointed out the other three Piru members inside the dorm.

"Alright, line up for chow!" shouted Mr. Grebel, standing at the end of the dorm with the door wide open. All the juveniles stood in a single file line, waiting for permission to proceed. "Forward march."

The juveniles quietly walked over to the chow hall. Once inside, they grabbed their trays and walked in front of a hot bar, where other inmates were serving: hot dogs, French fries, green peas, cherry pie and two milks. Everyone sat down and enjoyed their meal. Soon after, Solomon and Crab Crusher were issued: a camp number, bunk bed, clothing and fire gear.

At three o'clock, all the inmates that were out working forestry, returned to the camp. Twenty minutes later, the four fire crews returned also. Papoose introduced Solomon and Crab Crusher to all the Bloods that were in the camp. After the four-p.m. count, everyone enjoyed dinner, which was: Fried chicken, rice with gravy, greens, dinner rolls and German chocolate cake, with milk.

Juveniles were given recreation to burn off calories. They have access to the free weights, pull up bar, basketball court, handball court and C-dorm, to write letters or polish boots. Solomon went to C-dorm to write two letters, one to his mother and the other one to his grandmother, to check on them. Solomon went as far as to, ask his mother to come up to the camp and visit him. He also told her how much he loves and misses her. He mailed the letters off and fell asleep listening to 'Choosy Lover,' by the Isley Brothers.

November 18, 1987   Thursday 3:15 p.m.

TEN

Today is a typical day in Southern California, sunny and warm; this is usual for November. Chinadoll is sitting on the couch in the living room, puffing on a Newport cigarette, chasing it with a can of beer, while nodding her head to the song 'Rumors', by the Timex Social Club.

She notices the mailman walking into her yard with several pieces of mail. Chinadoll just received her crazy check two weeks ago, so she knows it's not any money. Plus, no one writes to her, so it had to be some bills. The mailman shoves the letters into the mailbox, that's attached to the front of her house.

"Kyle, come and get the mail!" yelled China over the music.

Moments later, Kyle sprints from his room to get the mail. He returns handing her the letters, then goes back to his room. Chinadoll looks at the first letter which is a gas bill and tosses it onto the coffee table. The next one was some coupons from Two for One Pizza; she tossed the coupons on top of the gas bill. The last letter was from Solomon. Her heart begins to pound uncontrollably as she noticed his name on the letter. She took a deep breath then exhaled, mumbling foul language, as she opened the letter. The letter read:

Chinadoll,

How are you doing? Fine I hope. This is your son, Solomon. I know we are not the best of friends, but we're family. I'm currently housed in Camp Louis Roth, in Tujunga, California. I'm gonna be here for the next nine, to twelve months fighting fires and working on my G.E.D. I'm going to study hard so I can pass the test and send it to you in the mail, so you can be proud of me, like I am of you. I admire and look up to you momma. The holidays are coming up; can you, along with: Kyle, Sabrina, Deena, and Grandma come up to see me? It would be much appreciated, because I love and miss you guys dearly. Write back, when you receive this letter.

Solomon W.S.P/R-130's

Chinadoll had mixed emotions after reading the letter. She read it two more times, to make sure she was reading it correctly. She mumbled a few bad words as she shoved the letter back into the envelope; tossing it onto the table on top of the gas bill and coupons. She fired up another Newport cigarette and started singing along with the song that's playing from the stereo, which is, 'She's Strange,' by Cameo. Thirty minutes and four cigarettes later, Chinadoll's singing was interrupted by the knocking on her screen door. "Who is it?!" she shouted, already knowing who it was, when she saw her daughter walking from across the street.

"Deena!" Deena responded, looking through the screen door at her mother.

"Come In!" Chinadoll approved, as she sang along to 'Weekend Girl', by the S.O.S Band. She pretty much knew that her daughter was coming over to start some type of conflict. So she prepared herself mentally.

Deena stormed in, sporting a pair of fire engine red stretch pants, that looked painted on, with matching sandals, and tank-top. She walked over to the stereo to turn it down a little, so that she can hear. Then stood in front of her mother with one hand on her hip, and the other one waving a letter in front of her. "We got a letter from Solomon today."

"And," Chinadoll added, with an attitude.

"He wants us to come and see him. He also told me to make sure that you come because he loves you," Deena explained becoming teary eyed.

Chinadoll took out another cigarette, from the pack of Newports that were on the coffee table and fired it up. She took one long drag from the cancer stick, blowing out smoke rings in a tandem. "I got a letter from him too."

"Where?" Deena inquired in disbelief, spotting the letter on the coffee table.

"Right there in your face. Pick it up and read it you nosy heifer, you know you want to," Chinadoll ordered, looking at her daughter through the cloud of smoke as she picks up the letter reading it.

After completing the letter, Deena shakes her head in disbelief. "So, what are you gonna do? We plan on seeing him for Christmas, are you coming with us?"

"I'm trying to figure out, why you be so damn concerned about Solomon? Out of all your brothers, you be extra concerned about him. I wonder why?" Chinadoll pried, staring Deena in the eyes searching for an answer. "You protect him like he's your man or something."

Deena's heart fell into her shoe from that statement. She's hoping that her incest activities with Solomon went unknown. "I protect him, because you disrespect him."

Chinadoll chuckled. "Yeah right. I was once your age too. I know your little hormones will get the best of you and you got to find something to hump on. Maybe Solomon was your outlet when I wasn't looking. Although I don't give a flying fuck."

Out of guilt, Deena dropped the letter back onto the table. "Look, are you coming with us or not?" She asked switching the topic.

"We'll see, maybe I will, maybe I won't. I'll let you know after Thanksgiving if I'm going," Chinadoll stressed, disposing the cigarette into the astray on the coffee table.

Deena figured that this was the perfect opportunity to leave, before her mother start prying into her past sexual relations with her brother. "Alright well, I'm going back home. I'm going to write him back and let him know that we're coming, with the possibility of you showing up." Deena replied, as she exits out the front door.

"Tramp," Chinadoll mumbled underneath her breath, as she watched her daughter sashay across the street.

Chinadoll stood up to stretch, then walked over to the front screen door to get some fresh air. Several cars sped up and down 129th Street blasting rap music. Klown walks past the house, with a red nose pit bull that has a red bandana around his neck. He sees Chinadoll standing in the doorway and acknowledges her, by flashing a gang sign in the shape of a P, she returned the gang sign. He kept strolling towards Avalon Blvd.

Just as Chinadoll was about to walk away, she notices a brand new black 500SL Mercedes Benz, pulling in front of her residence. She noticed that this was the same vehicle who picked up Solomon about a month ago, as the Benz was parking Chinadoll noticed a gray Crown Victoria cruising by in the same direction looking suspicious. Chinadoll frowned, as the bronze skinned beauty stepped out of the vehicle, dressed in a pair of black slacks, with the matching long sleeve silk shirt and high heels. Mrs. Milano removed her Chanel shades from her eyes, placing them on top of her head, as she entered through the yard's front gate, making her way towards the front door. "Um, may I help you?" Chinadoll inquired, trying to put a name to the unfamiliar face.

"Yes, hi, my name is Mrs. Milano. I am Solomon's 6th period school teacher. I was stopping by to check on him, he hasn't been to class in over a month and I was wondering was he okay, he is one of my best students," Mrs. Milano confessed, hoping that she could get some information out of his mother, because she doesn't believe the stories Tina-Ru has been telling her.

"Yes, he is okay. If you would like to notify him, he's at Camp Louis Roth, in Big Tujunga," Chinadoll stated. "Were you the person who came by to pick him up about a month ago?"

"Yes, Ma'am, that was me," Mrs. Milano confirmed. She already knew what type of woman Chinadoll was, from the stories Solomon told her. So, she knew how to communicate with her to get the information that she needed, so that she could look out for her boo.

"If you don't mind me asking, where did you take him that night?" Chinadoll asked, becoming a little jealous.

"No ma'am, I don't mind. I took him out to eat at a restaurant in West Hollywood called The Hungry Tiger. I was hooking him up with a film producer who was doing a documentary on gangs," answered Mrs. Milano.

"Don't you have to get permission from his legal guardian, being that he is under age?" Chinadoll inquired.

"Yes ma'am, that was our next step, but I wanted to make sure that he was okay with it first, being that he is going to be informing the media," Mrs. Milano shot back.

"Well you know, we don't do no informing around here, that's too close to telling," Chinadoll refuted, with a serious look on her face.

Mrs. Milano nodded her head in agreement. "I understand where you're coming from ma'am. If you don't mind me asking-"

"Yeah, I'm from Piru also." Chinadoll interrupted, reading her mind. She knew by the constant staring of all the red attire she has on, what was on Mrs. Milano's mind already. "My son was born into this gang culture. His step father was a well-known and reputable Piru member. However, his life was cut short by some racist officers who dropped him off in a rival Crip neighborhood on purpose, because he ran from them while under the influence of P.C.P. I can't stand the police. I hate them muthafuckas with every breath that I take. Fuck em'!"

"Mrs. Milano didn't know how to respond to her statement. But she felt her pain in every word that she uttered. She searched for a word to console Chinadoll, as she saw a tear slide down her cheek. "Ma'am, is there anything that I can do to help?"

"Yes, make sure the same thing doesn't happen to my son," Chinadoll wept, looking Mrs. Milano in the eyes, sniffing.

The statement gave Mrs. Milano a strange feeling. She wasn't sure if Chinadoll was giving her permission to adopt him or what. So, she answered with caution. "You have my word on that. I'll do everything in my power to make sure Solomon is looked after in any situation."

Chinadoll flashed a warm smile at Mrs. Milano, watching her as she adjusted the shades on top of her head. The brightness from the sun, caused the three karats in Mrs. Milano's ring, to dance in Chinadoll's face. "I see someone is looking after you, huh? You're sporting a nice size rock and pushing a new five hundred. What does your husband do for a living?"

Mrs. Milano almost peed on herself from China's question. She didn't wanna deceive Chinadoll about her husband's occupation; but she also knew the hatred she instilled for them, for setting her husband up to be murdered. So, she quickly changed the subject. "Outside of my teaching job, which I love to do; I'm also a real estate investor. I have several rental properties throughout southern California."

Mrs. Milano's plan worked. Chinadoll was quickly thrown off from her real estate statement. On top of that, the telephone started ringing in the background. Chinadoll looked over her shoulder at the telephone, undecided if she wanted to answer it or not.

That was Mrs. Milano's cue. "Ms. Spencer, I don't mean to be rude, but I must attend to some business ventures," she lied, walking off.

Chinadoll quickly ran to the phone inside the kitchen, snatching it off the receiver. "Hello! Hello! Whoever this is playing on my phone go and fuck yourself you scary ass bitch!" Chinadoll vented, as she slammed the phone back onto the receiver, watching Mrs. Milano climb back into her vehicle through the kitchens window. Chinadoll quickly ran from the kitchen out the front door to catch Mrs. Milano. She was a second too late, the black 500SL Benz sped off down a 129th street. Then it dawned on Chinadoll who Mrs. Milano was. *Oh shit! That's the wife of the muthafucka who had China killed! Now she's trying to get my son! My   baby!*

November 28, 1987   Sunday 10:05 a.m.

ELEVEN

It's been two weeks since Solomon and Crab Crusher arrived at Camp 15 and so far, it has been rough for them physically. The morning workouts are kind of strenuous being that the two were out of shape. But what really killed them, was the first time they hiked Kill 'em Quick Mountain. From a distance, they were convinced that they could make it up to the top in thirty minutes or less, which is the required time when you are in shape. Like countless other juveniles, it took them both well over the required time limit. In addition, they both tossed their cookies when they finally made it to the top.

The second time they hiked the mountain, they both made it to the top in thirty-three minutes, which was passable. Then they both passed the written exam on the first try. Now that they have knowledge of firefighting and the physical strength to fight it. Tomorrow they're both gonna be placed on fire a fire crew, where they will be on stand-by to fight a fire.

Solomon is alone, laying back on the grass by the basketball court getting fresh air, watching a five-on-five game amongst the juveniles. The temperature is around sixty-six degrees, with a slight wind breeze, which is known as the 'Santa Ana' winds. Solomon has been in two fights so far, both with Compton Crips. There's three more he vowed to fight, when the opportunity presents itself.

"Spencer, camp number thirty-two you have a visit," announced a voice, over the camp's loud speaker. Solomon sat up, making sure they were talking about him. Several Pirus that were on the basketball court stopped playing and looked over at

128

him. Crab Crusher were amongst the hooligans on the court, he threw his hands into the air. "They said me homie?"

Crab Crusher nodded his head. "On Piru homie, they called you."

"Townsend, I'm giving you a downgrade for gang talking," stated Mr. Noble, a heavy set African American man in his early forties. He is one of the staff members on duty sitting in a chair, overseeing the juveniles while they're at recreation. He looks over at Solomon, verifying that they called him over the camps loud speaker.

"Hey Spencer, they called you."

Solomon jumps onto his feet and walks over to Mr. Noble. "I wasn't expecting a visit, is there any way that I can take a shower?"

"Um yeah, go into your unit and break it down for a shower. I'm going to move my chair over there by the weight pile, so I can supervise the shower and basketball game," explained Mr. Noble, quickly moving his chair by the lower part of the weight pile.

Solomon quickly walked off to the unit. In a matter of seconds, he was walking out of the unit with a towel wrapped around his waist, toothbrush in his mouth, soap dish in his hand, and a face towel on top of his head.

Mr. Noble saw him as he exited the dorm. "Go ahead Mr. Spencer and shower. Remember, you still only get three minutes."

"Alright," Solomon responded, as he dashed into the bathroom, turning on the showers. He squirmed his body, underneath the Luke warm water, while rubbing himself for approximately one minute. He then stepped away from the powerful stream of water, lathering himself up with 'Irish Spring' soap; for another minute. Once his body was covered with soap suds from head to toe, he stepped back underneath the water rinsing off. A minute later, the water shuts off scaring the shit out of Solomon.

"Alright Spencer, you're done get dressed," demanded Mr. Noble, who was the culprit behind the water being shut off.

Solomon chuckled. "Alright here I come." He quickly dried off, then returned to his dorm to get dressed. After applying deodorant underneath both arms, lotion all over his body and Blue Magic grease into his hair, he put on a pair of new blue jeans and matching shirt. The only thing that was out of place, were his shoes. His personal shoes were confiscated, because they had colors in them. The only tennis shoes permitted in this camp, are all black ones. So Solomon must go to his visit in his work boots. He doesn't mind, the only thing that he's thinking about, is seeing his mother Chinadoll, along with his grandmother, twin sisters and Kyle's punk ass. *Who else could it be out there to see me? I knew my mother would come, if I asked her to come along with the rest of the family.* Solomon couldn't wait to hug his mother. He knew that this was the beginning of a mother and son relationship that's long overdue.

Alright Spencer, let's go. Your family is out there waiting on you. Don't have them out there waiting any longer than they have too, demanded Mr. Noble, waiting for him at the front of the dorm, with the door wide open.

"Here I come," said Solomon, reaching the door with a huge smile on his face.

"Have a good one now, ya hear?"

"Alright, thanks Mr. Noble," Solomon replied, as he walked towards the visiting area. Camp Louis Roth is small, so the distance between the two areas, is only about thirty feet; but to Solomon whose heart is beating out of control, seems like it's his last walk to the electric chair.

He finally reaches the hot dog stand looking office and instantly gets searched by Mr. Polaski, a short dwarf looking white man, with a napoleon complex. He orders Solomon to remove his shoes, then takes them and slap em' against each other, then gives them back to him.

"Alright, Mr. Spencer, your visitor is at table three, underneath the shed," said Mr. Polaski, pointing in the direction of his visitor. "She came late, so you're only going to have about thirty minutes of visiting time."

Solomon has perfect vision, but has trouble focusing in on the one person sitting at the table alone. He sees no red clothing, so he knows it's not his mother. As he gets closer, the woman sitting at the table waves at him. Solomon forms a huge smile on his face, when he notices that it's Mrs. Milano. She stood up with open arms inviting him to hug her. All the juveniles out there visiting their families, stopped to see who Mrs. Milano was coining to visit. Solomon hugged Christina like they were lovers reuniting. When he tried to let go she squeezed him harder, not letting go, rocking from side to side.

"I miss you so much Solomon," Mrs. Milano whispered, into his ear. Seconds later, she let him go smiling at him profusely. "Sorry that I'm late, here sit down."

Solomon sat in the chair, scooting up to the table. He just stared at Mrs. Milano in disbelief of her being there. "In a hundred years, I wasn't expecting you to show up. Although, you're here, I still can't believe it. How did you find me?"

"Your little girlfriend kept telling me that you moved and transferred to another school," explained Mrs. Milano out of jealousy. "I even drove through your neighborhood, and went to that skating rink that I dropped you off at, that night, searching for you. I finally grew the balls, to actually go to your mother's door, and ask her where you were."

Solomon eyes lit up, like a deer being caught by the headlights, of a vehicle. "You went to my house and talked to my mother?"

"Yep, I sure did," Mrs. Milano answered with a smile on her face.

"What did she say?" Solomon asked, curious to know how the two got along.

"Actually, she didn't give me any problems. I introduced myself to her as your teacher and told her that you were my best student. I told her I was worried about you, because I haven't seen you in over a month. So from there, she gave me your address," Mrs. Milano explained. Solomon nodded his head proudly of Mrs. Milano's courage. Cause he knows for real it could have gotten ugly. "I'm impressed."

"She was nothing like the person that you were telling me about. But she did brief me about your stepfather and those no-good officers that purposely got him killed. She also remembered that night, that I picked you up and took you to the Hungry Tiger. But once we became a little acquainted with each other, she was getting ready to pick me for information, but the telephone started ringing and that's when I made my escape," explained Mrs. Milano, who quickly changed the subject. "Here I brought you something to eat."

"What is it?" responded Solomon, looking over the plate.

Mrs. Milano removed the aluminum foil, that was covering the plate of food, that's sitting on the table. "I made you some homemade lasagna and garlic bread."

"Mmmm, Thank-you Christina," Solomon grinned, removing the plastic fork from the plate, taking several bites from the lasagna and garlic bread. Mrs. Milano looked on as Solomon closed his eyes savoring the taste. She formed a huge smile on her face. From his expression, it read gratification.

"I see they made you cut your hair off," said Christina, reaching across the table rubbing his head.

Solomon came up for air, to speak. "Yeah, it's mandatory. You can't fight fires with long hair."

"Were you upset?" Christina inquired, pouring him a cup of Dr. Pepper, from the two-liter bottle, that's sitting on the table.

"Yeah, but I can live with it. It'll grow back," said Solomon, in-between bites of lasagna. "I'm studying for my G.E.D, I should be taking the pre-test this Wednesday. Once I pass that, I'm taking the actual test so I can get my diploma."

"That's good Solomon, I'm so proud of you. I know you're gonna ace it on the first try," Mrs. Milano agreed, boosting Solomon's confidence.

After taking several more bites of lasagna, Solomon was finished. He placed the fork onto the plate, then washed his food down with the cup of Dr. Pepper, that was waiting for him on the table. He then sat back into his chair in deep thought. "You know, two weeks ago, I wrote my mother and grandmother and asked them both to come up here and visit me during the Thanksgiving and Christmas Holidays. I also told my mother in her letter that I'm going to pass my G.E.D test and send it to her, so that she could be proud of me. I didn't get a reply from neither party; so when they called me over the loud speaker for a visit, my heart was filled with joy, because I just knew that my mother was out here waiting on me. But-" Solomon drifted off in silence sitting up in his chair, placing his hands onto the table.

Mrs. Milano felt his pain of rejection. So, she consoled him by placing her hands, on top of his. I understand what you're going through Solomon. I know what it is like to feel neglected. Just give them a little more time, you still have Christmas coming up."

Solomon contemplated on her statement. "Yeah, you're right. I still have Christmas. But I'm not gonna hold my breath. In the meantime, I must get myself together, because I'll be eighteen when I come home; a grown ass man."

"Do you know what date you actually come home?" asked Mrs. Milano, anticipating the good news she has for him.

Solomon leaned back into the chair, rubbing his chin, feeling himself. "Yep, July tenth, on my eighteenth birthday. That's gonna be the best birthday gift, ever."

"That's perfect timing,"

"Perfect timing for what?" Solomon asked out of confusing.

"When your mother told me where you were located, I contacted Terry. That's who you're gonna be working with, when you come home. That's the documentary guy," explained Mrs. Milano. "And when you come home, don't worry about a place to live. I already have you an apartment waiting on you, fully furnished."

Solomon smiled. "Oh yeah. Why?"

"Why ask?" Christina shot back. "Oh and the reason why I said it was perfect timing, because Terry said he's not going to start filming until August. But I did tell him that you are currently incarcerated. He understood."

"Why is it that, my mother has a car that runs and has nothing but free time on her hands, but she couldn't pile up the family, to come and see me? As oppose to a married school teacher and real estate investor, finding time to come and see me huh? Why? asked Solomon, looking into Mrs. Milano's eyes searching for an answer.

Mrs. Milano locked eyes with Solomon, searching through her memory bank for the right word. "Because I care about you Solomon. And when a person cares about someone, they let them know through their actions and not their words."

Solomon was lost for words. He sat in silence, forming a lump in his throat. "So, you're saying that you care about me?"

"Absolutely," Christina responded. "You know when I was conversing with your mother, she said something that left me a little puzzled. She told me what happened to her husband and how much she hates the police. Then she became upset and began crying. I asked her is there anything that I can do and she replied by saying, 'make sure the same thing doesn't happen to my son,' I was totally confused, by that statement."

Solomon shook his head puzzled also. "I don't know what she meant by that. I don't think she was dropping some kind of hint. But with her you never know.

"Alright everyone, visitation is now over with! Say your last good byes!" Mr. Polaski yelled, interrupting the visiting area. Everyone in the area stood up to hug and kiss their visitors good bye.

Mrs. Milano stood up from her chair, with her arms wide open, inviting Solomon to hug her. Without hesitation he sprang from his chair, almost knocking her down to hug her. Christina let out a sigh of relief, as he rested his head onto her firm 42D bust. She squeezed him tight, while rocking from side to side then pulled away from him. "What size shoes do you wear?"

"Um, eight and a half. Why?"

"I was bringing you some tennis shoes, but I wasn't sure what size you wore," explained Mrs. Milano, adjusting her burgundy velour, Christian Dior sweat suit. "What kind of tennis shoes and hygiene products do you need?"

"Get me some all black Nike Cortez or K-Swiss. For the hygiene, get me some Tone soap, Cocoa Butter lotion, Blue Magic grease, Colgate toothpaste and some Dial Roll-on deodorant."

"Alright, I'll drop it off before I head back home," Mrs. Milano stated, as they both slowly walked to the hot dog looking stand, where numerous other juveniles were waiting to be searched and sent back to their dorms. Mrs. Milano gives Solomon one more hug, then pecks him on the lips, as she walks off. "I'll be back in two weeks and I'll be the first one here next time, so we can have a longer visit."

"Okay," Solomon responded, getting at the end of the line, to be searched also. He watched as Christina jumped into her 500SL Benz and sped off down Big Tujunga Canyon road.

In front of him is Pork, from Village Town Piru, who stands at five-foot nine and weighs a hundred and ninety pounds, of muscle. Facial wise, Pork looks like the rapper K.R.S. One, from Boogie Down Productions; but with a much larger nose and nostrils. He earned his name as a youth, because of his resemblance of Porky Pig. Pork and Solomon knew each other from Centennial High School. He looked over his shoulder at Solomon smiling. Solomon already knew where he was going with this. "Blood, where I know that broad from?" asked Pork, being nosy.

Solomon chuckled. "Centennial."

"That's where I know her from, I knew that was her, but I wasn't sure homie," Pork stated, laughing. "Damn blood, you got it like that? She kissed you on the lips and everything homie, Damn!"

"Nawh, she's like my cool aunt or big sister," Solomon explained, hoping to throw Pork off. But he kind of knew that was gonna be impossible, the way he was stalking them. Solomon noticed him looking over his shoulder at them periodically.

"Yeah right, the way y'all was over there looking into each other eyes. She was looking like a damn cougar, hunting for prey," said Pork, chuckling. But on the low, Pork wish it was him. His ugly ass doesn't know what it's like, to be loved by a woman other than his mother.

Mr. Polaski searched Solomon and Pork, by having them remove their shoes, then patted them down. Both were clear of contraband and could go back to their dorms. The two walked off.

"Who was that moms?" Solomon asked, about Pork's visitor.

"Yeah, moms came up here to holler at her boy. Ya know?" Pork responded. "Man, to hell with my visit. I wanna talk about your visitor, that's more exciting. Me and moms wasn't talking about shit blood."

Solomon chuckled from his remarks, as they arrived in front of C-dorm. Many juveniles were still outside playing basketball, checkers and sitting around the picnic area, listening to the cassette stereo. "I'll tell you about it later blood."

Like an excited kid being promised a gift, Pork walked away blushing.

"Alright homie, I'll catch you tonight at the movies."

Solomon's visit had his mind racing. He went back to the grass area and laid back onto his elbows, in the same position before they called him for a visit. Solomon thought about his future and pondered on the question that Mrs. Milano asked a while back, as to where did he see himself in the next five years? He knew growing up in the house with Chinadoll was unhealthy. He promised himself not to return there.

Furthermore, if she doesn't reply to his letter, or come up and see him for the holidays he's through with trying to reconcile with her, for something that he didn't do. That goes for his sisters, grandmother and Pirus alike. If he doesn't get any love, he can't give any love. Period! That's the new motto he is living by from this day forward.

Solomon's thoughts were interrupted, by the sounding of the camp's bell being rung. This means that all activities must come to a cease in preparation for count.

All the juveniles walked to their number box, that's located in front of the main office to be counted. After count was cleared, a staff member gave a motivational speech to the fire crew, that is on standby. Five minutes later; all three dorms were given showers. Soon after, dinner was served, following a movie. After the movie was over, the juveniles were allowed to use the restroom before the lights went out. Solomon noticed Ms. Martinez walking into the dorm with stereo in hand, relieving the staff that's on now. Horny juveniles grab socks from their lockers, extra toilet paper and anything else that they can think of to catch semen with.

Ms. Martinez set her desk up, preparing to pull an all-nighter. She removed her coat, exposing her semi-firm, 38d bust, that's stuffed inside her dingy V-neck t-shirt. "Alright gentlemen, lights out in two minutes," she stated, looking around the dorm at

139

the horny toads already in their bunks, underneath their blankets getting money.

Solomon took one look at Ms. Martinez face, which is caked up with foundation and shivered out of disgust. The whole dorm reeked of cheap Avon perfume, within five minutes of her being present. Solomon climbed into the top bunk, pulling the blanket up to his chin, staring at the ceiling thinking about the kiss he received from Christina today.

"Alright guys, lights out. Everyone in their bunks," demanded Ms. Martinez, as she pressed play on the stereo. The intro to the song, 'Reunited,' by Peaches and Herb comes on. She walks over to the switch box, shutting off all the lights inside the dorm; then takes a seat at the desk. In every direction that she turned, someone was jerking off to her. Their perverted actions filled a void in her lonely life.

Solomon replayed the visit inside his head from start to finish, while listening to the greatest hits from Harold Melvin and the   Blue-notes;   until   he   fell   asleep.

February 24, 1988   Wednesday 1:45 p.m.

TWELVE

Ninety days has gone by and Chinadoll still refused to correspond through letter writing or visitation. Solomon was crushed, but he moved on by washing his hands with her and Kyle. As for the rest of the family, they still had a rapport. His grandmother wrote a letter explaining that she had no way of coming to see him, due to transportation but sent letters and cards to him through the holidays. Deena and Sabrina both sent pictures, cards and letters to him for the holidays also. However, Deena writes him on a regular basis, each time sending photos. Tina-ru, Kay-Kay, Smurf, Vanity and Nine sent Solomon photos from their hood day, which was on January 30th. January being the first month of the year, represents the one, and the thirtieth day, represents the thirty, which equals a hundred and thirty, which stands for their denomination of Pirus; the Rolling 130's.

Keeping her word, Christina comes to see Solomon every two weeks, each time bringing a different home cooked meal. He can't wait to come home, especially to his own furnished apartment she promised him. The first thing he's gonna do is fuck Mrs. Milano in every room twice, until she taps out. He has a hundred and forty-one days left and counting.

Solomon has been on work restriction for the past six days, due to a ruptured Achilles heel that happened during a work detail, at a fire station in Pasadena. He along with two other juveniles who are sick, sits inside the dorm under staff supervision watching boring ass stories. Solomon came up with a clever idea, being that everyone was vacant from camp at their work detail; to go and pay the nurse a little visit.

"Ms. Wiley!" Solomon yelled, from his twin size, single bunk that he was given, when he was put on restriction.

"Yes, Mr. Spencer, how can I help you?" asked Ms. Wiley, a thirty-year old, five foot-four, African American woman, who looks like a baboon in the face; but has a curvaceous figure that a man would pay top dollar for.

"Can you call the nurse and tell her that I need to see her? I ran out of pain killers and my shit is starting to hurt," Solomon explained, trying to sound convincing.

"Alright, hold on, let me give her a call," stated Ms. Wiley, picking up the phone from the receiver on her desk, and calling her office. Three rings later, Ms. Crutchfield picks up the phone. "Ms. Crutchfield, I need to send Mr. Spencer to your office to see you. He's in dying need of pain killers. Okay, I'll send him."

Solomon already knew the light was green to go. He slowly pulled himself up using one of his crutches.

"Well, I guess you overheard the conversation. She said come on," Ms. Wiley stated, clowning.

Solomon snickered, as he slowly walked out of the dorm. *Good looking out bitch! I'm about to get my nuts out the sand!* Solomon thought to himself. For an injured person, Solomon was moving fast. He is long overdue, since he was promised to get 'anything' from the nurse in the time of need, when he first arrived here. As he reached the bottom of the stairs, he put both crutches in one hand, while grabbing the handrail with the other one and hopped up the flight of stairs, with his good leg, like a man with two good ones.

Ms. Crutchfield pushed the door outward with force, scaring the shit out of Solomon. "You got here pretty fast for a handicap."

"You must have been waiting by the front door for me, huh?" Solomon asked, with a smirk on his face. He knew she had an attitude with him, because he never followed up on his promise to stop by.

"What do you need?" she asked in a firm tone, cutting him off.

"I need some pain killers," Solomon responded, putting both crutches underneath his arms, walking through the front door.

Ms. Crutchfield held the door open for him until he made it inside. She then walked behind him slowly, as he secretly cased the vicinity for other staff members. Once he realized they were alone, he slithered into her office; she followed, closing the door behind her, leaving it ajar. Solomon took a seat on the operation table. Ms. Crutchfield leaned up against the sink, fondling her micro-mini braids, pulling them into a ponytail, with a holder, that she had wrapped around her wrist. "So, what type of pain are you in?" she asked, folding her arms across her chest, exhaling.

Solomon answers her question by staring into her eyes; once they made eye contact, he looked down at her bust. She formed a half ass smile. "Come here, check it out."

"Look boy, I don't have time to be faking. What kind of pills do you want?" Ms. Crutchfield asserted, in a firm tone. Out of all the promises made from other juveniles, none of them went this far; she instantly became moist. "Nawh, I'm serious. Come here," Solomon demanded, squeezing the bulge, that's forming in his crotch area. She slowly walked up on him. When she got in arms reach, Solomon grabbed her by the arm, snatching her in closer to him. "Bring your ass here, I ain't playing with you. I told you blood this Piru."

"And", she responded, sarcastically.

"Oh, I know what you like. You like to be dominated, huh? You must do, because you got a smart-ass mouth," Solomon explained in a firm tone. He then grabbed her by the bottom of her jawbone, with his right hand, until his hand slowly slid across her jaw, causing her lips to protrude, resembling a fish. Solomon then stuck his tongue into her mouth, kissing her passionately. Ms. Crutchfield pussy became so wet, her juices flowed down both legs, signifying that she was panty less. Solomon pulled her nurse uniform up her waist, exposing her nappy haired pussy and pink pussy lips that hung from her vagina like someone with severe hemorrhoids. Solomon rammed three fingers inside her birth box, covering them with her juices; then shoved all three fingers into her mouth. Ms. Crutchfield sucked her sauce off his fingers, like she was sucking the barbecue sauce from one of Mr. Jim's ribs. She wrestled with the button fly opening of his crotch area, until she finally grabbed a hold of his stiff member devouring it. Solomon was in heaven. She took his cock out of her mouth and slapped the head of it against her jaw and mouth spitting on it, then sucking the head dry. Solomon could no longer take it. He jumped off the operation table and bent her over it, then slowly entered her from the back and beat the pussy up, while she covered her mouth with both hands. Ms. Crutchfield grunted and growled, with every powerful stroke he dished out. As he felt himself about to cum, he sped the strokes up, like a race car in its final lap. He then grabbed her by the base, of her micro-mini braids and pulled, as he shot life into her. Ms. Crutchfield squeezed his dick dry, with her pussy muscles. "Aw, shieeet."

"Hurry up, we gotta get dressed," Ms. Crutchfield stated, by quickly pulling down her skirt, fixing her braids and opening the window into her office. She reaches into the pill cabinet and hands him a bottle full of Motrin.

"Alright thank-you," Solomon mumbled, shoving the pills in his front pocket while tucking his shirt back into his pants.

"No, thank-you Mr. Piru," she shot back smiling. "That was some good loving. That's what I needed."

"That's what we call Piru Love," Solomon joked.

"Oh, yeah? I'm feeling that Piru Love. I hope I could get some more before you go home," expressed Ms. Crutchfield, loosening her braids from the ponytail that it was in.

Solomon chuckled, as he grabbed his crutches, placing them underneath both arms exiting her office. "Alright, I'll see you later."

"Byyeee," chimed Ms. Crutchfield. Solomon's aggressiveness, made her fall deeply in love with him.

Solomon made it out the main office and stood at the top of the stairs. He notices two fire trucks speeding up the driveway, entering the camps ground. As Solomon stepped down the stairs, he missed one and fell. His body banged every stair stopping at the last one. Solomon just laid there silently, as the two fire trucks came to a screeching halt. Juvenile passengers in the back of both trucks, doubled over in laughter while the foremen from both trucks jumped out to aid Solomon. The banging of the stairs, also got Ms. Crutchfield's attention. She slowly walked to the bottom of the stairs, to give Solomon some medical attention. However, the two of them already knew what caused it. He was weak at the knees.

March 14, 1988   Friday 12:45 p.m.

THIRTEEN

Today would've been Chinadog's thirty-eighth birthday. Chinadoll along with Kyle, Deena and Sabrina, pulls into the driveway of her home, with a red bandana attached to the antenna, of her white 1976 Chevy Impala. She drove down Rosecrans Boulevard, waving her bandana from her antenna, hoping that she would've ran into some Compton Crips, so she can get her first homicide, with her brand-new Taurus 9mm. Although, Rosecrans Boulevard runs through one Piru hood after another, from Main street, all the way to east of Atlantic Boulevard. Crips occasionally, like to slither through and catch a Piru slipping every now and then. There's only one Crip neighborhood that is surrounded by Pirus, and that's the Santana Block Crips, right off Rosecrans and Santa fe Avenue.

Chinadoll and her children, departs her vehicle dressed in red clothing, from head to toe. They stand in the front yard and watch, as one vehicle after another, finds a parking space on a hundred and twenty-ninth street. In a matter of minutes, the whole block was flooded with Pirus throughout the greater Los Angeles County. Well known bloods from Athens Park, Miller Gangsters, Bounty Hunters, and Denver Lanes showed up, to pay homage to Chinadog also.

An hour ago, everyone met up at the Compton Cemetery, to visit China's gravesite. One Blood after another, put a red rose on his tombstone, then blew marijuana and P.C.P smoke over his grave, drenching it with: Olde English 800, Malt Duck, Night Train, Silver Satin, Seagram's Gin, and Remy Martin. The Pirus became

147

so deep and rowdy, the police were called, forcing the hooligans to celebrate elsewhere.

"Hey China, can we throw a barbecue in your yard?" asked Nine, as he rolled his wheelchair into her driveway. He already knew that Chinadoll would okay anything that has something to do with her husband's remembrance. But out of respect, he was going to ask because Chinadoll is his big home girl.

"Yeah blood on Piru, you know I ain't tripping. Let's do it," Chinadoll approved, walking into the backyard. Moments later, she returned pulling a huge homemade barbecue pit into the driveway. "Blood, go to Al's and get some ribs, steaks and links."

"Alright, bet," Nine responded, spinning his wheelchair in the opposite direction, preparing to get everything that they need to have a successful function.

"Blood, tell everybody to come inside the yard!" shouted Chinadoll, to no one In particular. Out of respect, everyone piled into the back and front yard of China's residence, leaving a few stragglers hanging alongside the front yard's fence and sidewalk.

Thirty minutes later, Nine and five other Pirus returned with: Ten slabs of ribs, one hundred steaks, one hundred hot links, one hundred hot dogs, two trash cans full of forty ounces, two trash cans full of sodas and one trash can full of bottled water. Deena and Sabrina helped by making bowls of potato salad and deviled eggs. Within the next hour, the function was in full swing.

Everyone was eating, drinking, and smoking. Rap and R&B, blared from Chinadoll's pioneer system, while two dice games occupied the driveway. The Pirus enjoyed themselves for hours, with no problems.

*****

Everyone enjoyed themselves until they were exhausted. Cholo from Campanella Park Pirus, broke up the dice game for $3,500 and gave Chinadoll a thousand-dollar cut. Nine showed Chinadoll some love, by giving her a knot of hundred dollar bills that totaled a thousand dollars, before exiting the function. Several other Pirus contributed money to Chinadoll, as they departed the shin-dig. When it was all said and done, she pocketed forty-five hundred, tax free dollars, in which she quickly stuffed inside a shoe box, in her closet. There were still well over five slabs of ribs, fifty steaks and cases of bottled water left over. After the last Piru member exited the yard, Chinadoll flopped down onto the couch inside the living room, collecting her thoughts. Deena and Sabrina brought all the extra food inside the house, wrapping it up in plastic and aluminum foil, storing it away inside the refrigerator and freezer. Kyle drug the barbecue pit and trash cans into the backyard.

"Sabrina, come hook this stereo up for me blood," ordered Chinadoll, firing up a Newport.

"Alright, hold up," Sabrina answered from the kitchen. Moments later, she began assembling the sound system.

"Ain't none of y'all heard from Maurice?" asked Chinadoll, taking a long drag from the cancer stick.

"Nope," Sabrina responded.

"Oh, his ass done went to his other family and he just said fuck us, huh?" Chinadoll blurted out. "I wouldn't be surprised, if they turned his ass out."

As if on cue, a black 1977 Buick Regal pulls in front of Chinadoll's residence. Inside, are two occupants removing their hats. Maurice exits the passenger side of the regal, and walks through the front gate of China's yard, dressed in an all blue khaki suit, and matching suede Pumas. The driver of the Regal leaves the car running out of nervousness, just in case.

Deena, who is washing dishes in the kitchen; notices Maurice walking towards the front door, through the window. She can't believe her eyes. She runs out of the kitchen, into the living room, with suds covering both hands. "China!"

"What? Dammit!" Chinadoll blurted out, becoming upset. She didn't notice Maurice on the other side of the screen door looking in.

"Look, Look," Deena whispered out loud, pointing at the screen door in disbelief.

"Momma...Momma," Maurice repeated, inviting himself inside of his old residence.

Chinadoll, Deena and Sabrina, looked at Maurice stunned. They couldn't believe he had the audacity, to come back to the neighborhood dressed like that; not just the hood, but to their house, on his father's birthday on top of that.

Maurice feels the tension getting thicker by the second. He just stood by the door, just in case he had to make a run for it. "Momma, I came by to see what y'all was doing on Pop's birthday."

Chinadoll's blood was boiling. "What the fuck do you mean, what are we doing on bloods birthday, fool?"

150

"We're doing, what we've been doing for the past three years; celebrating," added Deena. "What we're trying to figure out is; what happened to you, blood?"

Maurice's attention was on his sister Deena. Chinadoll stood up from the couch slowly walking towards Maurice. Maurice quickly switched his attention back to Chinadoll, to hell what Deena was talking about, he knew his stepmother was much more dangerous.

Through the living room window, Chinadoll can see Kyle slowly walking towards the front door. Kyle stares at the unfamiliar 77 Regal for a moment, before walking into the house. As he walks inside, he notices a startled Maurice. Kyle frowns at the sight of his brother's new allegiance. Kyle looks over at Chinadoll who is frowning; once he makes eye contact with his mother, she nods her head, giving him the green light to take off.

"Hey Kyle, what's up bruh?" Maurice inquired nervously, extending his hand out to Kyle expecting to get a handshake.

With the swiftness of a snake, Kyle struck Maurice in the jaw, causing him to bump his head against the wall. Maurice was too scared to let himself get knocked out, because he may never wake up again. Out of fear he tried to rush his brother. Kyle back peddled swinging wildly, catching Maurice in the face dazing him. Chinadoll walked up on him and struck him in the back of the head hard, with her nine millimeter.

Maurice burst through the front screen door, knocking it off the hinges screaming, "Mooommmaaaa! Momma, please!"

"Bring your bitch ass here, blood!" yelled Chinadoll, as she ran behind Maurice, chasing him through the front yard. He was so scared, that he tried to run through the front gate, which was closed, knocking himself onto the ground. Deena, Sabrina and Kyle stood over him and took turns stomping the shit out of him. Maurice curled up on the ground, screaming like a woman in distress. The occupant of the Regal saw the commotion, and burned off, leaving Maurice to die. Chinadoll, realizing that they were together, ran out into the street and fired several rounds, until his back windshield collapsed. She walked back into the yard with gun in hand and stood over Maurice. "How dare you come over here, and spit in our faces like, this? Get up and get your crab ass up outta here, blood!"

With that statement, Chinadoll's children stopped the assault on their brother. They backed away from him breathing heavily.

Maurice slowly rose to his feet disorientated. He looked at his stepmother and siblings, in disbelief of what they just did to him. He began crying. "What did I do to deserve this y'all? Huh?"

"That's probably what your father was saying, when the crabs were shooting him blood," Chinadoll declared, not feeling any sympathy for Maurice. She honestly felt that he totally disrespected everything that his father stood for. So, she threw it into his face, as a reminder that he grew up in a Blood household. "I don't know how you go over there and get turned out, in a matter of six months. This Piru blood until the casket drops, fool!"

"I came to pay my respect to my father," Maurice wept. "Fuck you blood!" Chinadoll vented, spitting in Maurice's face. "You came over disrespecting. Get up outta here before I bust on you blood. On Piru!"

Deena walked up on him and tried to slap him, but he blocked it while covering his head. Sabrina kicked him in the ass and Kyle followed up with an over hand right to the back of his head. This time Maurice cleared the fence with one hand, running down a hundred and twenty-ninth street with one shoe on horrified. Kyle grabbed his other shoe and tossed it into the middle of the street. They watched as their brother turned crab run   into   the   sunset.

June 18, 1988   Tuesday 7:00 p.m.

FOURTEEN

Like a proud mother, Mrs. Milano sat in the audience amongst other juvenile families, anticipating Solomon's name being called. Today is graduation day, for everyone who earned their G.E.D.'s. Solomon finally passed his test about a month ago. He would've gotten it much sooner, but his injury slowed him down from studying.

"Solomon Spencer," announced Mr. Nobel, standing by the podium. Solomon limped up to Mr. Nobel, accepting his certificate. Solomon turned to the crowd of visitors, searching for Christina. Mrs. Milano stood up with a camera. Solomon stood still, while holding his hand so that she could get a picture. After she snapped history, he walked off.

The ceremony was short, being that only ten people graduated. Afterwards, the graduates and family members were allowed to have dinner with each other, out in the visiting area. Solomon and Christina sat at a table in the far corner, enjoying each other's company. The two dined on fried chicken, macaroni & cheese, greens, cornbread and Pepsi, compliments of Camp 15's dining hall.

Mrs. Milano caused a lot of heads to turn, due to her black leather Moschino knee high boots, with matching painted on Guess jeans, that exposes her curvy thighs and ass, along with a black long sleeve Guess shirt. Her flat ironed hair that's down to her shoulders and back praises her MAC lip gloss and Maybelline eyeliner. She also flosses an 18-karat gold, woman's Rolex, with a diamond dial and bezel; while her three karat diamond earrings and wedding ring, dances from the sun's reflection behind them.

"Did you send your mother a copy of your G.E.D certificate?" Mrs. Milano inquired smiling.

"Nawh, I sent it to my grandmother. She wrote me back and told me how proud she was of me," Solomon responded, looking at Christina from head to toe out of admiration. "I see why everyone keeps staring at us, you're looking like something to eat"

Mrs. Milano pretended to play stupid, from Solomon's statement. "What are you talking about?"

Solomon smiled. "You know what I'm talking about. All eyes are on us; not only are all the juveniles and their visitors staring, but the men staff at this camp are drooling over you too."

"Well, they can look all they want, as long as they don't touch. Besides, I wore this so that you can enjoy it," Christina stated, playfully touching Solomon on his nose with her forefinger smiling.

"If you keep dressing like that, they're gonna realize that you're not my mother," Solomon hinted, wiping his mouth with a napkin. "I'm glad I come home next month, cause they're gonna figure us out sooner or later."

"You have twenty-two days left" Christina responded proudly, keeping count of his out date down to the actual day." Do you want me to come here and pick you up or what?"

"Oh, I forgot to tell you. I have to go back to court, to get released." Solomon explained.

"What? Go back to court? How come? You'll be an adult." Mrs. Milano asked, becoming upset.

"Yeah, I know, that's what my case manager told me. But look on the bright side, I haven't been in no trouble, plus I earned my G.E.D so there's no reason for him to not let me go," Solomon explained, but he knows that if he was messing up, he could get sent to a ninety-day observation at the California Youth Authority in Norwalk, California.

Christina exhaled, gaining her composure. "Well, I'm proud of you for accomplishing your G.E.D. Let's just hope that, the judge will be too. If you want, I'll come to the courtroom and speak on your behalf." Solomon flashed a warm smile. Mrs. Milano is everything that he wishes his mother was to him; except a cold-blooded freak, that he knows she is on the low. "Have you talked to Terry?"

"Yes, I have and he asked about you. I told him that you'll be coming home soon. He said that he can't wait to meet you."

Solomon nodded, looking around the visiting area. "Yeah, I can't wait to meet him too."

"This documentary could change your life for the better. Solomon I can't wait, until the day you start filming. I know that it's gonna be a huge success, I can feel it."

"You never know, this could be a stepping stone to a successful career huh?" Solomon added.

"Yeah maybe," Mrs. Milano answered, smiling. She noticed that Solomon is picking up weight. She reached across the table squeezing his bicep. "Have you been working out?"

Solomon looked at his bicep forming a muscle, making it tight for Christina. "Yeah, I'm back driving, they wouldn't let me for a while, because I was on restriction, because of my injury."

"What size pants and shirts do I need to get?"

"Thirty-two thirty, in the pants. In the shirts extra-large."

"I'm going to buy you an outfit to come home in, then we'll go shopping together, so you can get what you like. Alright?"

"Yes, ma'am," Solomon responded, in a joking manner.

Ms. Milano glances at her watch. "Well, it's about that time. I have to head back to the house, so I can prepare for school in the morning." She and Solomon stood up. "Alright, I should leave here on July ninth and more than likely, I'll go to court the next day. Just call Los Padrinos on that same day to see what my status is."

"Alright, baby, give me a hug," Christina demanded, reaching over to him, hugging him. "I may come on the first weekend of next month, but if I don't; don't sweat it.

I will definitely be there, on the day of your release." "Alright", Solomon responded, walking Christina to her car, which is parked on the campgrounds. He gives her one last hug and kiss before departing.

As Solomon makes his way to the recreation yard, he notices Ms. Crutchfield staring at him from the camp's office window with her arms folded. The look sent chills down his spine, so he quickly looked away. Since their first rendezvous, the two have been meeting every two weeks to get their freak on. Ms. Crutchfield's nose is wide open and she wasn't feeling Mrs. Milano one bit. Solomon noticed Pork and Crab Crusher sitting in the picnic area engaging in small talk so he picked up the pace, hoping that she doesn't call him. He successfully makes it to the area, flopping down onto one of the tables catching his breath.

"Blood you a fool," Crab Crusher stated, chuckling, as he cracked all his knuckles on both hands. "What have you done now? I seen you walking back to the Benz and kissing her. That's your bitch, huh?"

Solomon chuckled. "Nawh, she's more like a mother or cool aunt to me."

"Yeah right fool. That bitch is feeling your ass. She comes up here twice a week bringing food, shoes and anything else that you can have on a regular basis. I wish I had it like that blood on Piru," Pork stated, looking away becoming upset.

Crab Crusher looked at Pork with a look of confusion. "Anyway, we both getting short blood. I know you're gonna beat the pussy up when you get out huh?"

Solomon smiled hunching his shoulders. "I don't know, we'll see if the opportunity presents itself."

"That's a bad bitch homie. I'll pump one up in her if I was you blood," Crab Crusher expressed. "And we're both getting short. How many days you have left homie?"

"Twenty-one days and a wake up," Solomon responded, smiling.

"Damn, I'll be glad to see you go. When you leave, I'll have twenty days left homie," Crab Crusher explained, smiling exchanging handshakes with Solomon. "What are you gonna do on your first day out?"

Pork interrupted with envy. "Fuck the shit out of that school teacher. Keep it real blood you love that bitch huh?"

Crab Crusher looked at Solomon with a smirk on his face, then burst into laughter. "Nawh, I think you're more infatuated with her than blood is."

Solomon chuckled. "For real."

"I ain't gonna lie. I tried to sneak into the graduation so I can stalk her. I saw her when she pulled into the parking lot and sashayed to the auditorium. That bitch shut the whole camp down blood on Piru," Pork added grabbing his crotch.

"Yeah, they were tripping homie. I tried to slide in there, but they weren't having it. Mr. Nobel said that it was only for the graduates and their families," Crab Crusher explained, rubbing his hand across the top of his head.

"Shit, it wasn't but ten of us and out the ten, four of us were black. It was three Mexicans, two whites and one Asian. And on top of that, I was the only homie. The other three were crabs, "Solomon explained.

"Man, that one dark skinned crab from Bompton (Compton), had some thick ass hoes come up here to his graduation," Crab Crusher expressed. "What crab hood that fool from in Bompton?"

"Blood from Barver Mark (Carver Park)," Pork replied, frowning in the face, as if it left a bad taste in his mouth.

"That fool don't say nothing to me, he doesn't even look my way. He's the only crab from Bompton, I haven't got down with yet," explained Solomon. "I'm going to knock him out when I get a chance."

Pork chuckled. "I don't know blood, that fool got hands homie. I was in Bentral (Central juvenile hall) with blood and one of the homies from Water Front jumped out there and got clowned. We had to pull that crab off the homie."

They all burst into laughter.

The ringing of the camps bell, causes all activities to come to a cease. All the inmates stood on their individual numbered square, in front of   the office, to be counted. After the inmates were counted, they were given their nightly motivation speech.

"Spencer, I need to see you in my office," stated Mr. Waldorf. This is Solomon's case manager, a five-foot nine, white male in his late thirties.

"Permission to step away from the square sir," stated Solomon.

"Permission granted," responded Mr. Waldorf.

Solomon stepped away from his numbered square, quickly running up the stairs reaching the top. The look on Mr. Waldorf's face, gave Solomon a negative vibe. Mr. Waldorf opened the door and walked into the main office; Solomon followed behind. Once inside, Solomon flopped down onto the couch, exhaling. "What's up Mr. Waldorf, are you gonna finally let me use the phone?"

Mr. Waldorf exhaled. "Yes, um. You need to call your grandmother's house."

"What happened to my grandmother?" Solomon asked, becoming upset.

"I wasn't sure if anything happened to your grandmother. A woman called and left a message for you to call your grandmother's home," Mr. Waldorf explained, pushing the phone to Solomon. "Dial nine, then the number."

The palms of Solomon's hands become sweaty, out of nervousness; as he dials his grandmother's number. After the second ring, Deena picks up the phone weeping hysterically. "Hello."

"Deena what's up? This Solomon, what's going on?" Solomon inquired, becoming nervous. He knows it must be something serious, by the way she's crying over the phone. He prays that it's not his mother.

"THEY KILLED KYLE!" Deena yelled, as she began to cry hysterically, she then started screaming like a mad man. "THEM MUTHAFUCKERS KILLED

MY LITTLE BROTHER! ON PIRU BLOOD, IT'S ON! ON P-FUNK BLOOD! ON PI-MUTHAFUCKING-RU! THIS SEEKAY ALL DAY, EVEN ON A HOLIDAY!"

Solomon's heart began to beat uncontrollably from the news of his brother. He knew this was the wrong time to talk to his sister, so he hung up distraught.

"Would you like to make another call?" asked Mr. Waldorf, trying to console Solomon. He knew beforehand about his brother's death, because Sabrina called to the camp to relay the message. So instead of Mr. Waldorf telling him, he thought it would be better to hear it from the horse's mouth.

Solomon looked down into his lap, shaking his head. "No, thank-you, sir."

"You go home soon Mr. Spencer. What do you have planned, when you get out?" asked Mr. Waldorf out of concern. Many of his caseloads return to a former pattern of behavior, or get killed. He knew that Solomon was no different.

"I'm doing a documentary in August about gangs," Solomon explained, staring out of the window in the office.

"That's plan A. You need a plan B, C and D," Mr. Waldorf expressed. "Understand that, when you leave this camp, you'll be an adult. So, you're gonna have to start making adult decisions. You are the cause, of everything that happens to you, whether good or bad. That's the definition of responsibility, remember that."

"I will," Solomon responded, standing up from his chair. "Thank-you for the phone call Mr. Waldorf."

"No, problem," Mr. Waldorf replied, as he stood up from his chair.

Solomon walked out of the office, in route to C-dorm; pissed off. He opens the front door to the unit. "Permission to enter."

"Yes come in," Ms. Wiley ordered, smiling.

Solomon slowly walked to his bunk and sat down. The dorm was on low chatter, which allows juveniles to watch TV, write letters, shine boots, iron clothes and basically do what they need to do, before the lights go out. Papoose from Luders Park, strolls over to Solomon's bed area.

"Blood, what's happening? I thought you was going to the hole," Papoose stated, squatting down, resting his arms on both of his knees. He can see that Solomon is in deep thought. "Blood you bool (cool)?"

"Nawh blood, I got a disturbing phone call. My brother got smoked homie," Solomon replied, looking at Papoose rubbing his chin.

"Nawh blood, you bullshitting," Papoose responded, hoping that Solomon was joking.

"On Piru blood," Solomon shot back, with a serious look on his face. "My sister wrote me a letter a couple of months ago and told me that my brother Maurice came back to the house, with a flue (blue) khaki suit on; on the day of his father's B-day. She said that her; her twin sister, my brother Kyle; the one that just got killed and my mother, beat the dog shit out of him. So it probably was him and his homeboys."

"What crab hood your brother turned?" Papoose inquired.

"Barver mark (Carver-Park)," Solomon shot back, disrespecting the gang.

"Damn blood, that's fucked up. On Piru we can kick something off with these crabs in the dorm. I don't give a fuck," Papoose signified, showing some Piru love.

Solomon saw the seriousness in Papoose's face and smiled. He respected his gangster; Solomon shook his hand, ending the shake by interlocking their hands in the form of two P's. "Nawh blood, I appreciate it. It wouldn't do nothing but hurt me, I go home in twenty-two days homie. But when I get home it's on and cracking."

"Ten minutes before the lights go out gentlemen," Ms. Wiley announced, to the dorm.

"Alright homie, I'll get with you in the morning blood," Papoose said as he stood up.

"Alright Piru," Solomon responded, as he stood up from the bed.

All the juveniles grabbed their towels and toothbrushes, heading out the door, to use the restroom. Ten minutes later, everyone is squared away underneath their blankets, in their bunks. Ms. Wiley turns out the lights inside the dorm and presses play on the stereo's cassette deck. 'Tender Love,' by the Force MD's comes on, crooning the hooligans to sleep; while the other perverts jerk off to Ms. Wiley, who's loving every minute of it.

Solomon prays for his brother's soul silently, as he stares at the dorm's ceiling. He then ponders on his release date, and how he's gonna avenge his brother's death. He also thinks about how Christina is more of a mother to him, than Chinadoll. His mind races, until he drifts off to sleep.

June 25, 1988   Tuesday 7:00 p.m.

FIFTEEN

Four hours ago, Kyle was laid to rest at the Compton cemetery next to his father Chinadog, in Compton California. There were so many Pirus in attendance, one would think that Kyle was a reputable Piru member. However, his reputation and status with the Pirus, didn't ring bells past his bedroom. The Pirus paid their respects because, they knew that he was a product of Chinadog and Chinadoll and was more or less born into his affiliation. Kyle was dressed in true gang fashion. He sported a steel gray suit, with a burgundy shirt, tie, shoes and a burgundy bandana neatly folded in his suits pocket. The funeral service was held at Mt. Calvary Baptist Church, on the corner of El Segundo Boulevard and Towne Avenue. In attendance, were the Carson Sheriff, to make sure there were no retaliations. Since Kyle's death, four Compton Crips were killed, in the surrounding areas.

Chinadoll is not a heavy drinker, but today was a special occasion. This is her second plastic cup of Seagram's gin and Super Socco citrus juice.

Chinadoll is starting to feel lonely; Kyle is dead, Maurice turned crab, and Solomon is locked up. Deena and Sabrina can't deal with Chinadoll too long, before their attitudes clash with one another.

Chinadoll nods her head to the song, 'Sunshine' by Alexander O'Neal. Three songs later, she falls asleep on the couch.

*****

"China, get up! get up!" Deena ordered, pulling on her mother's sweat shirt.

China woke up incoherent. "What's up blood?"

"Blood, change your clothes. I'm going around the corner, to get the g-ride (stolen car) by the time I get back, you should be dressed and ready. Be standing outside too, Deena demanded, dressed in an all-black, tight fitting body suit and matching high heel pumps. Deena walked out of the house in route to get the vehicle.

Chinadoll walked into the bathroom and splashed cold water onto her face; waking herself up. After taking a good stretch, she felt relieved. She removed her red clothing, replacing them with a black sweat shirt, black tight fitting Levi jeans and black K-Swiss tennis shoes. She wrapped her hair up into a bun, then grabbed her Taurus 9mm, placing it in her waist, covering it with her sweat shirt. After she placed on her woman's leather gloves, she walked out the house. Perfectly timed, Deena hit the corner, pulling alongside the curb in front of her mother, in a black 1988 Nissan Maximum. Chinadoll climbed into the passenger side of the vehicle, seconds later, they sped off into traffic.

"Blood, what time is it?" Chinadoll asked, placing on her leather gloves removing the 9mm from her waist.

Deena glanced at the clock inside the dashboard. "Nine forty-five, blood."

"Let's do a complete circle and hit every crab hood in the vicinity, starting with the McKinley's," Chinadoll explained.

"Alright", Deena responded, getting caught at the stoplight on Avalon Boulevard and El Segundo Boulevard. This gave her enough time, to place on her black leather gloves. She quickly reached over her mother, opening the glove compartment, removing a 9mm and a box of shells.

The light turns green, the Nissan Maxima sped north on Avalon Blvd.

They reach a hundred and twenty-first street, making a right turn into the Crip's territory. Both Piru members looked for anyone slipping, as they drove up and down every street, with guns in hand. "Blood, I don't bee (see) nothing."

"Go through their hood one more time, if we don't bee nothing, go through the Barvers," Chinadoll ordered, ready to unload her handgun in a crab's chest.

They double back and saw nothing. They drove east on a hundred and twentieth street, in route to the Carver Park Crips territory. This is the hood Maurice is from now. The vehicle reaches Antwerp Street and makes a left turn. They cruise the block looking for a victim. Upon reaching the corner of a hundred and eighteenth street, they spot three Crips running up to several cars selling weed and crack.

"Blood, let me go first. Bust a C.K. and park down the street. I'm going to walk up on these fools." Chinadoll explained, putting a bullet inside the chamber.

"Bet" Deena responded, following her mother's orders. She drove to the next corner and parked.

"Keep the car running blood, I'll be back," Chinadoll ordered, stepping out the passenger's side of the vehicle, tucking the gun in her waist. As she gets closer to the Crips, she becomes nervous. It's been a while since Chinadoll put it down. But when she do, she gets her man.

One of the Crips watches China as she approaches them. She had to think of something fast to rock these fools to sleep. "Hey now, let me get a bag of weed baby."

Once the Crips heard a female's voice, they let their guards down. One short stocky built Crip, ran up on Chinadoll excited. "What's up baby, what you need?"

"A dub sack of weed," Chinadoll ordered, reaching into her back left pocket pulling out a wad of bills.

"Damn baby, I don't have no dub sacks, all I have is dime bags," the short stocky Crip explained. "Hold on, let me see if Reese has it. Hey Reese, you got some weed cuz?"

"Yeah, hold up homie!" Maurice yelled from a distance, running to his stash spot to get the bag of weed.

Chinadoll's heart started beating uncontrollably. Her mind began to race, as she made her decision, as to how she's going to put her move down. The short stocky Crip had his back towards Chinadoll. Slowly, she removed the gun from her waist, hiding it behind her right leg. Chinadoll waited, as Maurice jogged in her direction. She wanted to personally shoot him in the face, because she felt that he had something to do with Kyle's death; retaliating for the beat down that they handed him, on his father's birthday.

The short stocky Crip turned towards Chinadoll, as Maurice became feet within the two. With her left hand, Chinadoll handed the short stocky Crip a crispy twenty-dollar bill. When Maurice noticed his stepmother, he also noticed the grim reaper. He tried to speak, but his brain couldn't register the words fast enough. Chinadoll shot the short stocky Crip in the head one time, dropping his lifeless corpse onto the pavement hard. The other Crip took off running. Maurice tried to turn around and run, but was hit multiple times in the lower back and ass. He fell onto the sidewalk on his stomach.

"Momma please, don't! Pleeeaassee! Momma! Dooon't," Maurice screamed, as he squirmed on the sidewalk.

"Fuck crabs, this Piru, blood," Chinadoll stated firmly, hitting Maurice in the back twice, bringing his movement to a cease.

"Ca-riiippp!" the other Crip shouted, before letting off three rounds at Chinadoll, who hid in-between two parked cars. There was a moment of silence, as the Crip tried to inch his way towards Chinadoll, who came from in-between the vehicles letting off numerous rounds at the Crip, while dashing towards the black Maxima. The Crip began firing numerous rounds at Chinadoll, as she climbed into the passenger side of the car, ducking in the front seat. Chinadoll quickly began putting shells into her clip, while Deena exited the vehicle ducked down, creeping alongside the car in high heels, waiting on the opportunity to return fire. The gun fire came to an end.

"Deena, get back in the car, don't shoot. Come on blood. On Piru before One Time comes," Chinadoll pleaded, nervously stuffing her clip with ammunition.

Deena jumped back into the car and cruised off slowly, until she reached Central Avenue, in which she made a left turn. As the Maxima passes the intersection on a hundred and twentieth street, sirens can be heard wailing from the direction of the crime scene.

169

"Blood, I shot Maurice," Chinadoll replied, in a firm tone, looking at her daughter.

"Did you kill him?" Deena inquired, looking her mother in the face, waiting for an answer. She reminisced on when they were growing up, how China used to favor Maurice over all the children, on the simple fact that he was Chinadog's first son.

"I don't know, I put one in the other crab's head; when he saw him drop, he took off running. I hit him in his back and ass, as he fell onto the ground," Chinadoll explained, with a smirk on her face. "Then blood started yelling; I got pissed and fed him two more in the back, shutting his ass up."

"Were you trying to kill him?"

Chinadoll thought for a moment, pondering on the question." Yeah, because I felt like he spit in our faces."

"Well, so be it," Deena responded, switching the conversation. "Blood, I'm about to go to the liquor store right off Central and Compton Boulevard, next to the Shell gas station."

"Yeah, I wanna see you put it down one time. See what you're working with blood," Chinadoll joked.

"I'm going to get out the car and put this ass on display watch," Deena marveled, as she entered the left turning lane that turns onto Compton Boulevard. The vehicle turns, then busted a C-kay (made a U-turn) parking in front of the liquor store. Deena removed her gloves. "Blood, I'm about to post up. Jump in the driver's seat."

"Alright blood," Chinadoll stated, "Get me a pack of Newports."

Deena stepped out the vehicle, thicker than a snicker, entering the liquor store. The man behind the counter was an African man, standing at six foot-four. He watched closely as Deena sashayed throughout the store. She reached inside the refrigerator grabbing a Super Socco citrus drink; then a pack of Newports when she reached the counter. Just as she was about to leave from the counter, two Crips strolled into the liquor store drawing attention to themselves, by making unnecessary noise.

"Damn cuz, look at baby with all that ass," Polo blurted out. Polo is a member of the Palmer Block Compton Crips, who stands at six-foot two and a hundred and ninety-five pounds. Polo is butter yellow in complexion, and sports his hair in French braids.

"I ain't never seen baby before cuz. She does have a fat ass though," Magic added, holding his crotch while gawking Deena's assets. Magic is a short fat dark skinned man, who wears a jheri curl.

Deena overhears the two potential victims, commenting about her backside. After she receives her change from the African, she grabs her items and struts pass the two Crips blushing.

"Damn baby, how can I see (be) down?" Polo asked, walking on the side of Deena blowing in her ear.

"You tell me," Deena responded, still walking towards the door. Polo stopped, Deena kept walking outside handing her mother the pack of Newports. "I got me one blood."

Chinadoll quickly removed a cigarette from the box and fired it up. "How you gonna get them? You don't have on any pants to hide the gat."

"I'm going to get in the car with them and have them drive me to Athens Park. Once we get over there, I'm gonna smoke their boots, Deena explained, with a huge smile on her face. "You're gonna follow behind us, blood."

The two Crips walk out of the liquor store. Deena walks away from the vehicle, sashaying towards the Crips.

"What's up baby you lost? Do you need a ride?" Polo asked, pushing up in Deena's face.

"Yeah, can you give me a ride?" Deena responded, in a pouty tone.

"Only if I can get your number," Polo shot back, aggressively.

"You got that?" Deena replied, blushing, while taking a few swallows from the citrus drink.

"Come on," Polo replied. The three of them walk to a beige, 1986 four door Caprice Classic, that's several feet in front of the vehicle that China is in. Deena gives Chinadoll a nod, as she climbs into the automobile.

"Where am, I taking you to?" Polo asked, as he started up the vehicle, and sped off into traffic.

"Um, drive down Compton Boulevard, until you get to Figueroa, then make a right," Deena explained, looking over her shoulder, out the back windshield. She can see her mother trailing behind from a distance.

Polo looked at Deena through the rear-view mirror. "Say, baby, what's your name?"

"Deena," she replied, smiling at Polo in the mirror.

"My name is Polo, this is my homeboy Magic," Polo explained.

"How you doing Magic?" asked Deena.

"I'm straight, I'm straight," Magic responded. "How you doing?"

"I can't complain, ya know? I was with this fool just a minute ago, and when I told him that I wasn't giving him the panties, he left me at the liquor store," Deena lied, trying to sound convincing.

"What set (neighborhood) was dude from?" Polo asked.

"I think he was from Piru, he used to say Tree Top all the time." Deena explained. "I'm not familiar with this gang stuff. I just moved to California about six months ago."

"Oh, is, that, right? Where you from?" Polo asked.

"I'm originally from Kansas City, Kansas," Deena responded, knowing that the two Crips would be thrown off, by the lie she was telling.

"So, I would assume that you're single huh?" Polo inquired, making a right turn onto Figueroa street speeding.

"Yeah. What about you? I know you have at least two broads huh? Deena stated, blowing smoke up his ass. She glanced over her shoulder, out the rear windshield, noticing Chinadoll still trailing' behind them.

Polo chuckled. "Nawh, to be honest, I'm not seeing anyone at the moment."

"So, if or when we hook up, I'm not gonna have to beat any of your bitch's ass am I?" Deena asked, getting Polo excited, as if he is about to get some pussy.

"Nawh, it ain't that type of party baby," Polo answered. "You sure you don't have a man? I don't wanna put myself in a position, where I gotta risk my freedom."

"Cuzz, look at them slobs (Bloods) over there at the gas station," Magic interrupted, pointing at the five car loads of gang bangers dressed in red attire, flashing gang signs at every passing vehicle. Polo's heart began to beat irregularly as they get caught at the light on Figueroa and Rosecrans Boulevard. "Aw Cuzz, don't trip, them fools are probably strapped. Just be cool. Hey, Deena where do you stay at?"

"Right off Figueroa and a hundred and twenty-seventh street, Deena replied, looking in the rear-view mirror at the expressions, on both of their faces; which showed terror. Both Crips knew that the area they're about to enter, belongs to the Athens Park Bloods, a well-known blood gang that has a reputation, for killing Crips in the surrounding areas. Deena knew that they may have some safety concerns, so she consoled them, by feeding them a lie. "Y'all don't have nothing to worry about, they don't be on the street I live on."

The light turns green, Polo drives off slowly; then picks up speed when he's out of view of the bloods. "Are you going in and out or are you going to get a jacket and come with us?"

"Um, I don't know. Where are you guys taking me, if I go with y'all?" Deena inquired, leading them on like she's naive.

"Shit, back to the hood to sip on some drink and blow some weed," Magic stated bluntly.

"What neighborhood do you guys live in?" Deena asked, playing stupid.

"We from Tragnu Park," Magic lied proudly.

"Well, I guess I can go with y'all. Y'all not gonna take me back to you guy's hood and run a train on me are you?" Deena inquired, putting ideas into their heads.

The two Crips looked at each other, thinking to themselves. *Oh, we got one!* "Nawh, we don't get down like that baby it's just us three. But later, we can get a room at the Motel on Artesia and Figueroa if you're down," Magic insinuated.

"Yeah, I'm cool with that. Cause when I get drunk, I sometimes blackout and I don't wanna wake up with a dick in my mouth, ass, pussy and both hands," Deena expressed, blowing their egos up, before she blow their brains out. They reach a hundred and twenty-seventh street. "Park on the other side of the driveway, in front of this beige house."

"Alright." Polo answered, following Deena's instructions. He turned the engine off, looking around nervously, checking his rear view and passenger door mirrors, looking for bloods. For some reason, there's not an Athens Park in sight.

"I'll be right back, I'm going to get me a jacket. It won't take me but five minutes," Deena explained, as she exited the four door Caprice. As she walks across the street, she enters an alleyway behind multiple apartment buildings, out of the Crips view. Chinadoll drives down a hundred and twenty-seventh street, first noticing the Caprice parked, then noticed Deena walking through the alley. Chinadoll sped around the block, to enter the alleyway on a hundred and twenty-sixth street. A minute later, Deena noticed her mother coming thru the alley from the other end. She pulls up to Deena. "Blood park the car."

"What you about to do?" Chinadoll asked, with her head sticking out the driver's door.

"Pull over and park blood," Deena demanded. The Maxima pulls over, turning out the lights. Deena climbs in on the passenger's side of the car. "Blood, I got them fools thinking they about to get some pussy."

"I mean shit, wearing the shit you have on, I would think that too," Chinadoll shot back.

"Man, I'm about to down both of those crabs," Deena expressed, as she placed on her leather gloves. She reached in the backseat, grabbing her all black Fila jacket, placing it on, and zipping it up to the neck. She then took her left arm out the sleeve, grabbing her 9mm, concealing it underneath the jacket. "Hey, I'm going to get back in the car with them and make them drive down Broadway. Once I past a hundred and thirty-second, by all those factories, I'm bodying their asses, on Piru."

"Alright, so I'm going to go post up on Broadway street right now," Chinadoll replied, starting the vehicle back up. Deena exited the passenger's side of the Maxima.

"Alright, be safe blood."

"I will," Deena responded, as she watched her mother exit the alleyway, making a left on a hundred and twenty-seventh street. Deena stalled for a moment, giving her mother enough time to clear the block, so that they wouldn't raise any suspicion. Deena then removed her right arm from the sleeves jacket, so she can appear to be cold as she exits the alleyway and into the backseat of the Caprice. "Sorry, I took so long. I had to get me a jacket, it's getting a little nippy."

"Aw you cool Deena, don't trip," Polo stated, as he started up the vehicle. While she was away, they debated on who, was gonna bang her first, and how. Polo puts the car in gear, turns on the stereo and drives off. The song 'Bass,' by King Tee comes on; Polo turns it up and the two Crips nod their heads in unison. This was perfect timing for Deena, who placed the gun on her lap, then put both of her arms through the sleeves of her jacket; slowly putting a bullet into the chamber.

There was no sight of Chinadoll, who took a short cut, to get to Broadway Street. Various thoughts ran through Deena's mind, as they turned onto Broadway Street, off El Segundo Boulevard. Deena searches for her mother, looking on both sides of the street. The next stoplight is on a hundred and thirty-fifth street. Deena is becoming a little frustrated. Then out of nowhere Chinadoll pulls up to the corner of a hundred and thirty-second street.

Damn, bitch! It's about time! Deena thought to herself. The beige Caprice gets caught at the stoplight on a hundred and thirty-fifth street. Deena glances over her shoulder, seeing Chinadoll slowly driving in their direction. Deena looked in all directions, in search of the police. The street is totally empty of any vehicles; Deena sees this as an opportunity to strike.

The two Crips are still nodding their heads, to the pounding rap tunes of 'Straight outta Compton' by N.W.A. Deena eases the 9mm inches from the right side of Magic's head, pulling the trigger twice. The force from the bullet, caused Magic's torso to fall into Polo's lap. The front windshield was covered with blood and brain matter. Polo screamed like a bitch, but was silenced when a bullet entered the back of his head, exiting out of his left eye socket. Polo's body slumped onto the steering wheel, causing the horn to wail. His foot slipped off the brake, causing the car to slowly creep into the intersection. Deena departed from the backseat of the Caprice, with gun in hand. Chinadoll pulled on the side of the beige vehicle; Deena ran around the car and jumped into the passenger's side. The black Maxima busted a C-kay and sped off; vanishing into thin air.

July 9, 1988   Tuesday 8:00 a.m.

SIXTEEN

Solomon gets butterflies in his stomach, as he and two other juveniles, patiently wait for their ride to pull up, to the camp, so that they can go to Los Padrinos juvenile hall. The other two juveniles with Solomon, have a similar situation. They must appear in front of a judge to get released, also.

Ten minutes later, the white van pulls into the camp's driveway. Solomon receives hugs and handshakes from all his Blood associates, as he departs.

The three juveniles load into the van. Solomon takes one last look at the camp, forming a smile onto his face, from the memories. The van speeds off and hops onto the freeway. The other two juveniles who are Hispanic, carries on in a deep conversation; while Solomon enjoys the warm weather and view. A lot of things are weighing heavy on Solomon's mind, the fact that he has to go back to court is stressing him out, because anything can happen. But the killer part is, he has to go on his birthday, spending a night in Los Padrinos, where a gang altercation is promised.

Thirty-five minutes later, the van pulled into the receiving unit at L.P. Even though the juveniles are coming from a camp, they still have to be processed as if they're new arrivals. Being that it's only three of them, the processing time was short. Under supervision, the three were walked to their designated units.

"Spencer," said the male staff member, looking at Solomon. "Stand in front of your unit's door."

Solomon stepped out of line and stood by the door, until a staff member let him inside.

"Hi, how are you doing? Have a seat until we get you a room," explained the male staff member.

"Alright", Solomon responded, taking a seat in the row of plastic chairs, inside the day room. Several rows behind him, are three Crips in conversation. Once the staff member is secured inside the office, the Crips see their opportunity, to investigate Solomon.

"Pssst...Hey, homie, where you from?" asked C-Mac, a high yellow, skinny built Crip, from Rolling Twentys, in Long Beach.

Solomon turned in his chair towards the three Crips. "I'm from West Side Piru," then turned away.

"This Rolling Twenty...Crip, Long Beach," C-Mac stated, with pride.

"This Santana Block Compton Crip," Gorilla-Dee added. Gorilla-Dee has the perfect name; everything about him physically, has the likeness of a silver back gorilla.

"This Original Swamps Compton Crip," Lamp joined in. Lamp is five-foot eleven, a hundred and ninety pounds. He's caramel brown, with a dried out jheri curl, with tattoos scribed all over his face, neck, and arms.

Solomon exhaled from stress build up, but remained silent. He didn't feel like going to the box (hole), so he let them get that off. But he knows it's not gonna stop there.

"Say, loc, where you coming, from?" C-Mac asked aggressively.

Solomon remained silent, keeping his composure.

"You hear us talking to you, cuz," Gorilla-Dee instigated.

Solomon, tired of the Crips shenanigans, turned in their direction. "Check this out blood; number one, I don't fuck with crabs. Number two; if any one of y'all have a problem with it; we can take it in the bathroom, and I'll knock one of y'all out, and stick my finger in your booty, blood."

Lamp smacked his teeth. "Alright, cuz, when they do showers I wanna see your work."

"Say no more," Solomon responded, turning back around.

The three Crips talked underneath their breaths, plotting on what they're gonna do to Solomon.

A male staff member walked into the day room. "Spencer."

Solomon stood up and walked up to the staff member. "Yeah."

"You are assigned to room ten," said the staff member, pointing down the hallway.

"Alright, thank-you," Solomon responded, walking down the corridor. He stepped inside of his room, looking around in disbelief. The first thing that got his attention was the smell, which smelled of anus and feet. Solomon slowly walked over to the chrome sink and toilet, looking inside; searching for the source of the smell. The toilet and sink is empty of any contents; so, he looked onto the walls furthering his search.

"Spencer here is a bedroll," said the staff, opening the room's door, handing him a bedroll.

"Excuse me, can you bring me some cleaning supplies, please?" Solomon asked, tossing the bedroll onto the table.

"Oh, yeah, it smells like ass in here. We had some fool in here that was smearing shit all over the walls and floors," the staff explained, rubbing the air passage of his nose. "I'll be back with something, to get rid of that shitty smell," explained the staff member, walking away.

The staff member returned with: Ajax, Pine-soil, a clean rag, a Brillo pad, a broom and mop. Solomon immediately went to, work, getting rid of the rooms foul odor. Twenty minutes later, the room was spotless, and ready to be occupied. Solomon made up his bed, then returned the cleaning supplies to the staff member. All the juveniles were called to the day room, in preparation for lunch. The unit orderlies quickly rearranged the tables and chairs around, while the rest of the juveniles came in from school, finding them a seat at the table. The orderlies placed one tray and milk, in front of each juvenile. Juveniles must wait until the staff member gives them permission to dine. Being that Solomon came from a fire camp, that served good food, the items in front of him seemed like torture. Today's lunch is one hot dog, chopped up into a small portion of baked beans, a milk, a salad, and two oatmeal raisin cookies.

"Alright gentlemen, eat," said the male staff member, in a firm tone.

Once given the word, hungry juveniles wasted no time scarfing down the items. Juveniles are not allowed to talk, when eating; however, after the meal, the unit can talk on low chatter. Some juveniles had to return to school, while the others had the privilege of going for half a day. After the rows of chairs were sat back up, in its original order; each juvenile found them a seat. Solomon sat in the front row alone. C-mac, Gorilla-Dee and Lamp sat in the last row, telling the other Crips who were at school, the latest and the greatest. They all frown at Solomon, who is unaware.

A tall brown skinned juvenile, with French braids in his hair, takes a seat next to Solomon, in the empty chair. This is Bad Habit, from West Side Piru.

"What's up homie? Where you from?" Bad Habit asked, while crossing his legs, placing his hands-on top of his knees.

"I'm from West Side Piru, Rolling One Thirties," Solomon responded, nonchalantly.

"What's up homie? I'm from the Four Line (134th St.). They call me Bad Habit," Bad Habit explained, extending his hand out to Solomon.

Solomon shakes his hand. "What's up Piru, they call me Solo."

"You just came in blood," asked Bad Habit.

"Yeah, I just came from Camp 15. I have to go back to court tomorrow to get released," Solomon explained, with stress written all over his face.

"Aw shit, you're alright homie. They're gonna let you out watch," Bad Habit expressed, trying to lift his spirits showing some Piru love.

"And the cold thing about it is, tomorrow will be my eighteenth birthday."

"Oh, yeah, they can't hold you anymore. You're not gonna even go to court tomorrow, watch. They're going to release you from here, homie," Bad Habit explained. "They just did the homie from Athens Park, like that."

"Man, I hope so blood," Solomon responded shaking his head in disbelief.

"Don't trip, watch, Bad Habit shot back. Hey, homie, did you have some words with one of them fools behind us?"

"Yeah,"

"Which one?"

"All them fools. They hit me up (asked) when I came into the Unit. After I told them where I was from, they call themselves banging on me," Solomon stated. Then I banged on all of them fools, so the tall fool said he wants to get a fade (fight) when they do showers."

"Is, that, right?" Bad Habit asked, looking over his right shoulder at the group of shit starters. "Don't trip Piru, don't trip. When we go to recreation tonight, I'll introduce you to the other homies. They're on the other side of the unit. We're the only Bloods on this side."

"Oh, yeah? Damn."

"Alright, gentlemen, back to your rooms. We'll see you guys later, around chow time," the staff member commanded.

All the juveniles dragged their feet, trying to avoid locking up in the rooms. Solomon and Bad Habit shook each other's hand, ending it with the signature interlocking p's, before locking up in the rooms.

Solomon flopped down onto the bunk, still stressing about tomorrow's court date. Over the room's speaker, the Isley Brothers, 'Groove with you,' comes on. Solomon laid down on the bunk with his arms behind his head, enjoying one Isley cut, after another. The music played until count time, which is four o'clock. After count chow was served, then the juveniles went out to recreation, for an hour. Afterwards, they went back to their rooms, to prepare for showers. The male staff is running the showers with an iron fist. So, Solomon has to take a rain check for the fight. After the showers were over, snacks were served, which was a slice of watermelon. The juveniles were given one more head call, before being locked in the room until tomorrow morning.

Solomon is excited as hell, to be back inside the room listening to Oldies. He is unable to sleep, so he does ten sets of push-ups, doing seven to ten reps each set; while listening to the: Dramatics, The Dells, Curtis Mayfield, and Teena Marie. When the song 'Young Love,' by Teena Marie came on, Solomon stripped down asshole naked and beat his meat. After he finished, he laid down   and   went   to   sleep.

July 10, 1988   Wednesday 7:00 a.m.

SEVENTEEN

"Happy Birthday to me, Happy Birthday to me!" Solomon sung, out loud. Today he is no longer a juvenile, and he can't wait until the judge cuts him loose. He woke up in the middle of the night with an erection, thinking about how he's gonna lap his tongue across Christina's asshole, toes, nipples, and pussy. He climbed out of his bunk, placing his clothes on, then began pacing the floor of his cell.

From a distance, Solomon can hear the unlocking of cell doors. He becomes excited, because he knows while breakfast is in session, court is also called.

"Alright, gentlemen, breakfast time. Come out, walk in the center of the hallway, with your hands behind your back," ordered the male staff member, firmly.

Solomon strolled down the hallway, until he reached the day room, which was already set up for breakfast. Solomon found an empty spot at the table and sat down. Bad Habit sat at the empty spot in front of Solomon. The two acknowledge each other, then gets permission from the male staff to begin eating. Solomon removed the plastic from his tray staring, at the contents inside: one boiled egg, two slices of bread and a small portion of oatmeal. To drink; one pint of low fat milk. Solomon told himself that this is gonna be his last meal ever, in prison. Without thinking about it, he put a dent in the meal.

"Alright, listen up, when I call your name, get ready for court: Brown, Chavez, Williams, Jacobson, Durant, Mendez,

Suddeth, Howard, Blake, and Smith," announced the male officer, overlooking the piece of paper in his hand.

Solomon's heart fell into his shoes. "Damn, blood," he voiced, becoming upset.

"What's your last name, homie?" asked Bad Habit, in a low tone.

"Spencer," Solomon replied.

"Excuse me sir, did you say Spencer?" Bad Habit asked the staff member.

The staff member looked over the list twice. "Nope, there's no Spencer on here"

"Alright, thank you," Bad Habit responded. "I'm telling you blood, you're getting out after four o'clock, watch." "Man, I hope you're right," Solomon stated.

"Oh, yeah, Happy Birthday blood," said Bad Habit shaking his hand.

"Good looking, homie," Solomon responded.

"You're gonna get a good birthday present later today, watch," Bad Habit explained.

The juveniles were sent back to their rooms, to prepare for school. Solomon had the option of staying in the room, or hanging in the day room. Since Bad Habit went to school for half a day, he thought it was wise to hang with himself in his room.

After taking a nap lunch was served. Solomon didn't feel like eating so he gave his tray to Bad Habit. Afterwards, some of the juveniles returned to school, while the others stayed in the unit. The staff allowed the juveniles that were in the unit, some leisure time in the day room. Solomon and Bad Habit sat in the front row of plastic chairs, having a conversation.

Bad Habit looked at Solomon's face and chuckled. "Blood, look at the bright side you completed a camp program, they have no reason to keep you. Plus, you're an adult, as of today."

"I also earned my G.E.D., while I was there," Solomon stated to Bad Habit, as if he was the judge.

"Aw, yeah, you're good homie. What court were you suppose to go to?"

"Judge Fletcher, in Long Beach?"

"Oh, trust me, you're good. But by you getting that G.E.D, just makes it much sweeter," Bad Habit explained, trying to sound convincing. "Shit, you should be grateful that you got action at going home. I'm facing life." "On Piru?" Solomon asked, with a look of seriousness on his face.

"On Piru, blood, I ain't going home. I'm fighting two hot ones (murders), on some erickets," (Crips) Bad Habit stated.

Solomon thought about his statement in depth, nodding in agreement. "I feel you homie, I feel you."

"You feel me homie? I understand what you're going through, but it's nothing like what I'm going through, blood," Bad Habit explained, with a serious look on his face. "So, whatever your outcome may be, you'll still be in a better position than me, homie."

"You right homie, I'm sweating some small shit, for real," Solomon replied, stroking his chin.

"When you get out, what are you gonna do?"

Solomon thought about the question before answering. "Bone my school teacher."

Bad Habit chuckled. "Your school teacher, you're bullshitting, right?"

"Hell nawh," Solomon responded.

"What school she teaches at?"

"The ten," (Centennial High School) Solomon stated.

"The ten?" Bad Habit asked, becoming excited.

"What's her name?"

"Mrs. Milano, she's an Italian chick that teaches history," Solomon explained. She only been there two years."

"Oh, okay, that's why I didn't know her. Shit, I never went to school no way," Bad Habit stated chuckling. "Alright, gentlemen, take it to your rooms," ordered the staff member.

All the juveniles slowly walked out of the day room dragging their feet, anticipating locking into their rooms. Solomon and Bad Habit gave each other a pound before going into their rooms.

Solomon went into his cell, and started pacing the floor for five minutes, thinking about the conversation he and Bad Habit shared in the day room, before getting exhausted and flopping down onto the bunk. For some reason, no music was playing over the loud speaker. So, Solomon reminisced about Ms. Crutchfield on how he used to beat them guts up, until he dosed off.

Three hours later, Solomon was awakened by the knocking of his door, by the male staff member. "Spencer! Spencer! Pack your shit, you're going home!"

Solomon jumped out of his bed, running up to the door, still half asleep.

"Excuse me sir, what did you say?"

"Pack your shit, you're getting released. I'll be back in five minutes," stated the male staff member, walking off down the corridor.

Solomon couldn't believe his ears, all that stressing he was doing, instantly went out the window. He dropped down to the floor, sticking his mouth underneath the door. "Hey, Bad Habit! Bad Habit!"

"What, you're out of here, huh?" Bad Habit asked, who already overheard the staff giving Solomon the news he was waiting to hear.

"Yeah, homie, I'm out of here. You knew what you were talking about."

"I told you homie, I seen the homie from Athens Park, do it," Bad Habit responded. "Go out there and enjoy yourself on your birthday, homie."

"Oh, you already know, homeboy," said Solomon, bursting into laughter.

"Hit it one time for me, Piru," Bad Habit expressed, speaking about him having sex with Mrs. Milano.

"You already know. I'mma make her chuck up the "P," one time for you homie," Solomon pledged.

"Alright, homie, much love," Bad Habit replied.

"Hey, homie, what's your full name?"

"Levert Cox," Bad Habit responded.

"Alright, homie, I got you. I'm going to shoot you some flicks, on Piru," Solomon promised.

"Spencer, let's go!" shouted the male staff member, down the hallway.

"Alright," Solomon shot back, standing back on his feet, stepping out of his room into the hallway. He quickly walked a couple of doors down, to Bad Habit's door window and flashed a Piru sign at him. Bad Habit returned the flashing of the "P" sign. Solomon strolled off.

"Hey! Stop gang banging and let's go!" the male staff member, demanded.

"I'm coming," Solomon responded, walking in his direction.

"Where is your property?" asked the male staff member.

"I don't have any, I sent it home from camp," Solomon explained, ready to get the hell away from there.

"Alright, let's do it," said the male staff member. As he and Solomon walk down the hallway, they make a brief stop at the unit office.

"Shall we keep the light on for you?" asked another black male officer.

"Who me? Hell nawh, today is my eighteenth birthday. My next stop if I come back, will be the L.A. county jail," Solomon explained, proudly.

"Oh, you'll be moving up in the big league, then," the black male staff replied.

"Alright, I got your card. Let's get you to the streets," said the male staff member.

Solomon and the staff member walked out of the unit, across the compound, finally making it to the receiving and discharging unit. The black male staff member, handed the Hispanic female staff member, his I.D. card and walked away.

The Hispanic woman overlooked Solomon's card. "Okay, Mr. Spencer, have a seat, and I'll bring you your dress out clothes."

"Okay," said Solomon, taking a seat in the row of plastic chairs, alongside the wall.

The Hispanic woman returns with a Nike box and a pair of stone washed Guess jeans and a matching gray, long sleeve Guess shirt. "Here, you go Mr. Spencer," said the Hispanic woman, handing Solomon the items. "Thank-you," responded Solomon, overlooking the clothes.

"Um, the dressing room is over there," stated the Hispanic woman, pointing in the direction of the room.

Solomon walks into the closet size room, closing the door behind him. He swiftly removed all his detention bureau clothing, including his socks and drawers. He opened the Nike shoe box; inside, was a pair of burgundy and gray boxers, a black Gucci belt, white tube socks, and a pair of black Jordans. He removed the plastic from the clothing and put them on. After he was fully dressed, he walked out of the dressing room smiling, as he took a seat in the row of plastic chairs. He's so excited, he constantly checks his Air Jordans for scratches.

"You look nice Mr. Spencer," flirted the Hispanic woman.

"Thank-you, ma'am," Solomon smiled.

"You're welcome," she shot back blushing. "You'll be leaving in a minute. I'm just waiting for them to give me the word."

"Alright...Thank-you," Solomon replied.

"Who is that lady out there waiting on you? If you don't mind me asking."

"I don't know, what did she look like?" Solomon asked, playing with the Hispanic woman.

The Hispanic woman thought for a moment, searching for the right word.

"Beautiful."

"Oh, that's my woman."

"Wow, she's nice. You're into older women, huh?" "Nawh, they're into me," Solomon shot back sarcastically.

"Oh, excuse me," she responded, turning up her lip.

"You're excused," said Solomon, smiling.

Their conversation was interrupted by the ringing of her telephone. She picks it up for a moment, then hangs it back up. "Are you ready Mr. Spencer?"

"Hell, yeah," Solomon said excitedly, springing from his chair. Solomon and the Hispanic woman walked from the receiving and discharging unit, down the corridor, finally reaching the front lobby of the Detention Bureau. Sitting alone, in the row of empty cushion chairs, was Christina holding a bouquet of roses in one hand, and several balloons in the other one, with a smile on her face.

Solomon has never been looked after like Christina has been looking out. He walks up to her giving her a bear hug, then pulled back and pecked her on the lips.

"Happy eighteenth birthday, Solomon," flirted Mrs. Milano, handing him the balloons and flowers. The look in her eyes, is saying that she needs a good fucking.

"Thank-you, Christina, I really appreciate it," Solomon expressed, accepting the gifts, smelling the bouquet of roses. "Oh, and thank-you for this outfit I have on too."

"You're welcome I know you appreciate it, that's why I did it for you Solomon," Christina cherished. "Do you like your outfit? I mean did I get the right clothes?"

"Oh, yeah, the outfit is perfect. I'm impressed," Solomon remarked, "You look nice, were you at some business meeting or something?"

Christina chuckled. "No, silly, I'm taking you out to a restaurant, for your birthday Are you ready?" asked Christina, who is dressed to the nines sporting a black skirt, with a matching silk shirt and six inch stilettos. Her lip gloss, compliments her hair that is cut into a bob.

"Yeah, I been ready, let's go," Solomon anticipated. The two walk from the lobby area, to Christina's black 500 SL, that is parked out in the front.

Christina opens the passenger's door for Solomon. "Thank-you, sweetheart."

Christina blushed. "You get royal treatment today...it's your birthday." She responded, closing the door, walking around to the driver's side, getting in. She started up the car and drove off. "I went to the DMV, and brought you back a driver's handbook. Study it, so you can get your license...Okay?"

"Yes, ma'am," Solomon responded, looking at Christina. "Where are, we going? If you don't mind me asking. I know we're going out to eat."

"First, we're going to the Del Amo mall, to get you some clothes. Then to the Redondo Beach Pier, to my favorite seafood restaurant. Afterwards, I'm taking you to your new apartment."

Solomon smiled, then reached over and kissed Christina on the cheek. She blushed profusely.

They arrived at the shopping plaza in twenty minutes. They went from one store to another, buying everything: shoes, pants, shirts, boxers, socks, belts, and fitted caps. The two spent a total of two hours shopping, then arrived at a low-key restaurant that sits on the pier, in Redondo Beach, California. They both dined on lobsters, shrimp and mussels, while enjoying breathtaking views of the Pacific Ocean. An hour and a half later, they were in route to Solomon's pad. The stressing from Los

Padrinos, shopping at the mall, and stretching the lining of his stomach, took its toll on Solomon putting him to sleep. Christina looked over at Solomon smiling, gently caressing the side of his face.

Christina's black 5OOSL turns off Western Avenue, onto a hundred and fifty-seventh street. Solomon wakes up, as the Benz pulls into the parking stall, in front of his new apartment.

"I'm sorry, I didn't mean to fall asleep on you like that," Solomon apologized, wiping his face several times, before becoming coherent.

"That's okay honey, we're home now. Here, grab your stuff, Christina ordered, stepping out of the automobile, removing a few bags from the trunk. She opens the door of the apartment, placing the bags onto the floor, returning to the vehicle, to help Solomon with the rest of his bags.

Solomon closed the trunk after removing the bags. He followed Christina into the apartment, closing the door shut with his foot, as he placed his bags onto the floor, looking around his fully furnished spot. "This is mine?"

"It's all yours honey. Happy Birthday," Christina responded, kicking off her high heels." Come on, let me show you around."

Solomon followed her down the hallway, as she opened the door to his bedroom. The room is equipped with a queen size bed, dresser drawer with a huge mirror attached to it, two night stands on both sides of the bed, with lamps; a twenty-four inch color TV and a stereo with a six disc, CD changer. They walk back down the hallway, opening the door of the bathroom, which was decorated in all red; everything from the face towels, shower curtain, soap dish, dry towels, floor rug, and toilet stool cover. Solomon smiled, loving how she decorated the bathroom. A few feet away is the kitchen, which is spacious, being that it's a one bedroom apartment.

"I love this apartment Christina, thank you very much, Solomon articulated, walking up to her sticking his tongue into her mouth, kissing her with aggression.

Christina replied, by jumping onto Solomon, wrapping her legs around his waist, and her arms around his neck, returning the aggression as she kissed. Solomon carried her petite frame down the hallway, into the bedroom, slamming her down onto the bed, removing her skirt, revealing her black g-string. "Hold on baby," said Christina, removing her silk shirt and underwear, propping herself up on her elbows. Take off your clothes baby.

Solomon is in awe, of Christina's beautiful bronze body. He follows her order, standing on the side of the bed removing his clothes, until he was completely nude. "Christina, your body is so beautiful," he complimented.

"Thank-you baby. Your body is gorgeous too. I guess it's true what they say about black men, cause your cock is fucking huge," Christina complimented. She had never seen an eight and half inch ham in person, let alone felt one inside her. She stuck two fingers inside her pussy, swirling them around, then pulled them out and inserted them into her mouth sucking off the juices. "Come and eat your birthday cake, baby."

Solomon slowly crawled onto the bed, like a panther circling its prey.

Christina parted her legs, inviting Solomon to munch on her freshly Brazilian waxed muff. Solomon is a professional cunt lapper, thanks to his twin sisters, so he knew what method to use, to get Christina going. First, he gently kissed the folds of her pussy, then inserted two fingers behind her pearl tongue, vigorously moving them from side to side, while sucking her clit. Christina closed her eyes placing her hands on the back of his head, bringing him in closer to intensify the feeling. Christina moaned in ecstasy. Solomon sucked, nibbled and licked on her pussy, until she couldn't take it anymore. Her head fell backwards, as her volcano started erupting. The orgasm was so good, her right leg shook uncontrollably. Afterwards, Solomon pushed her knees up to her chest and began swirling his tongue around the rim of her asshole. Christina couldn't believe the skills of this barely legal horn dog. A few revolutions later, he turned Christina onto her side, slowly sliding his mushroom head inside of her cum drenched pussy. Five inches later, stroking at a moderate pace, she was screaming like a white girl in a horror movie. With each stroke he added an inch, until her tight pussy gripped his entire length.

Once her coochie was broken in, he began ramming his pole in her from the tip, to the nuts at a rapid pace. Christina was confused, she didn't know if she wanted to keep screaming or start creaming. They went through various positions, in forty-five minutes; but their final lap, was when she rode him, until they both climaxed. They both laid in the bed, sweating profusely. Solomon is exhausted and Christina is in love. After taking a ten minute breather, they go for round two, which lasted another thirty minutes. Soon after they took a shower together, caressing and cleaning each other.

Christina lathered up the face towel, scrubbing behind his ears, neck, back and ass cheeks; she saw his cock swell up from her touch, so she wrapped the towel around his stick, stroking and cleaning it at the same time, while tongue kissing him. Moments later, they rinsed off and stepped out of the shower, dripping wet.

"Christina, this is the best birthday present that I ever had," Solomon explained, pulling the top down on the toilet stool sitting on it.

Christina blushed. "You had some cake, are you ready for some ice cream.?" "Yes," Solomon answered, not knowing what she really meant.

Christina walked over to the toilet, exchanging positions with Solomon. She sat on the commode, while he stood up. She grabbed the base of his cock, squeezing it, making it look like a swollen kielbasa sausage. She slowly circled her tongue around the tip of his head, while looking up at him, like the dirty little slut that she really is. Solomon smiled. She spat on the head of his dick several times, until it was dripping with saliva. Like a pro, she started bobbing on his pole at a rapid pace, occasionally gagging as it touched the back of her throat.

With both hands, she grabbed him by his butt cheeks thrusting him inside of her mouth. Solomon closes his eyes gently holding the side of her face, moaning. She grabbed his tally whacker with both hands, only covering seven inches. The remainder of his schlong hung out of her hand, like a foot long hot dog in a regular size bun.

With both hands she began twisting, lifting up his cock, sucking on each one of his balls. She then grazed her bottom

199

teeth underneath the head of his dick stimulating his v-spot. She extended her tongue from her mouth, as far as it would go, then began lashing it with his dick, as if it was a whip, while looking into his eyes. After bobbing and slurping on his pole non-stop, the insides of his butt cheeks started to tingle. Christina felt his dick head swell up in her mouth, so she kept her pace, until he shot his load into her mouth. Solomon's knees became weak, as she breathed through her nose, milking his hose of the last few drops of semen. She quickly stood onto her feet, grabbed Solomon by his face, and tongue kissed him, sharing his sour, salty, unborn baby eggs with him.

After they tongue wrestled for a minute, Solomon pulled away wiping his lips. "Uggh."

"There's your ice cream, baby," Christina stated, wiping the sperm from the corners of her mouth, tasting it. She glances at her wrist watch, not realizing how late it was. "Baby I have to go. It's getting late. I left you five hundred dollars spending cash, make it last...Okay?"

"Alright," Solomon responded.

Christina walked into the bedroom, Solomon followed behind. She began getting dressed. "Baby, I would advise you to study for your license, so you can start driving. I know you don't wanna walk or catch the bus, because it could be dangerous."

"Hell, yeah, I'm not doing no walking or public transportation," Solomon shot back, lying onto his bed, turning on the television, searching for something to watch. I'm going down there tomorrow, and apply for my license.

"Good, then we can go to the auction and get you something, until things get better," Christina explained, as she fixed her hair, by running her fingers through it. "Give me a kiss baby," she demanded, leaning into the bed. Solomon reaches up, and tongue kisses her.

"When are you coming back?"

"Tomorrow we have to go down to the phone company and get you a phone, and go grocery shopping," Christina responded, as she grabbed her purse and keys, walking towards the door. "Bye, honey, I'll see you tomorrow. Have a happy birthday."

"Alright, thank-you," Solomon responded, watching Christina as she walks out the door. Solomon exhaled, thinking about all the events that occurred today, from the time he woke up in that shitty room in Los Padrinos. However, he ended up getting his cake and eating it too. Although, he is done with his mother he thought about her, and wondered what she was doing. He was thinking so hard, that he became exhausted, and fell asleep.

August 6, 1988   Saturday 10:35 a.m.

EIGHTEEN

What Solomon accomplished in thirty days is more than what people twice his age accomplish in years. Solomon feels like a responsible adult now that he has his: driver's license, house phone, groceries and a used car. Now if he could land a job, he'll be complete.

Five days ago, Solomon and Christina met up with Terry concerning the documentary. The same day they met, Terry and Solomon hit it off and started filming within minutes of the meeting. Terry was impressed with Solomon's ability to articulate the life style of a gang member. But was moved when Solomon went in depth about his personal story of being born into the Pirus. Terry instructed Solomon on how to operate his hand- held video camera letting him borrow it, so that he could capture some footage and interview other Piru members in his neighborhood.

Today is Solomon's first time making an appearance in his neighborhood since he's been out of jail. He turns his beige 1977 Buick Regal, onto an empty a hundred and twenty-ninth street. He pulls alongside the curb in front of his grandmother's house and park; soon after jumping out his vehicle excited.

"Deena! Deee-nah!" Solomon shouted, walking towards the front door of his grandmother's home.

"Brother!" Deena shouted, out of excitement. She and Sabrina ran from the house dressed in flimsy red pajama top and bottoms. They both, along with their grandmother who were trailing behind them showered him with hugs and kisses.

"You've been out of jail for a month and just now coming to see us blood?" Sabrina inquired, rubbing her fingers through his short curly afro that's starting to grow back.

"Yeah, I had to get my priorities straight first," Solomon responded.

"Okay baby, it was nice seeing you. I'm going back in the house, these fools around here are shooting up everything," their grandmother stated. She walked up to Solomon giving him another hug and kiss, then walked back into the house.

Solomon and his sisters leaned up against his Regal. "So what's been popping around here blood?" Solomon inquired, looking in both directions of a 129th street which is completely empty.

"Man, it's been ugly around here blood on Piru," Sabrina stressed stroking on her freshly done micro mini braids. "Blood, it's good that you was gone for a while. Everybody is hiding out, going to jail or getting shot. They killed Kyle in the front yard blood. That's crazy."

Solomon looks in the direction of his mother's front yard, where Kyle was murdered. He looks in the doorway noticing his mother puffing on a cigarette, behind the screen door. He turns back around to his sisters. "Is she still tripping?"

"Aw man she's worse. After Kyle got killed, she went to the doctor and found out that she has been bi-polar since Chinadog was killed. Oh she be happy one minute, then stressed out the next. On top of that, I think that she's going through menopause," Deena explained, in a low tone chuckling. She grabbed Solomon by the hand, walking him across the street, to his mother's home. Sabrina followed behind. "China! Your son is out of jail."

Chinadoll stepped out into the front yard, taking one last drag from her cigarette, before thumping it into the grass. "What's up blood? We was coming to see you, but my car was broke," Chinadoll lied, blowing the remainder of smoke through her nose.

"You need to quit," Deena cut in putting her mother on blast. "You know damn well nothing is wrong with your car."

Chinadoll switched the subject. "Your school teacher came through here while you were locked up, wanting to know your address. I gave it to her blood, on Piru."

"Yeah, I know. She told me about it when she came to visit me," said Solomon, throwing it in her face.

"Oh is that right? She drove way out there to see you?" Chinadoll asked, becoming jealous. She can see that Mrs. Milano slowly took her spot and is not feeling it one bit.

"Yeah, she came to see me several times. Plus she came to my graduation and picked me up when I got released," Solomon expressed to his mother wishing it was her.

"So that's where you're staying at now?" Sabrina asked, being nosy.

"Well, I'm not staying with her because she's married. But she got me a spot in Gardena," Solomon bragged.

"Whuuut? Say it ain't so? You got it like that blood?" Deena asked, rolling her neck with her hand on her hip becoming jealous. She then took a look at him from head to toe. "Oh, so that's why you're looking all spiffy, huh?"

Solomon responded by hunching his shoulders, throwing his hands into the air. "Hey, what can I say?"

I wonder if she told him that her husband killed my husband, Chinadoll thought. "She's gonna pay you, then play you," she stated.

"Damn, we should have went to Centennial; maybe we could have came up on a sugar daddy like you came up on a sugar momma," Sabrina said jokingly. The twins were shuttled to Cleveland High School in San Fernando Valley, through a magnet program that allowed inner city children to get a better education in the valley.

"She's not a sugar momma. She has my best interest at heart. I look at her more like a mother," Solomon expressed, dropping a bomb on Chinadoll.

I bet she does have your best interest at heart. Both of y'all are crackers! China thought to herself, feeling stupid from his comment but remained silent.

"When are you going to invite us to your new apartment?" Deena asked, looking at Solomon with a devilish smirk on her face while stroking one of her braids.

Chinadoll watched Deena closely, she can see that they committed an act of incest in the past. "Nasty heifer," she mumbled underneath her breath.

"I'll invite all of you guys over there during the holidays that's coming up," Solomon stated, trying to throw a dust in

Chinadoll eyes. "Oh, I forgot to tell y'all. I'm filming a documentary on gangs do y'all wanna be in it?"

"Fuck nawh!" Chinadoll snapped, adjusting the red bandana that's wrapped around her head aunt jemima style. "What are you gonna do tell the whole world how we get down blood? What's wrong with you fool!"

Solomon shook his head in disagreement. "No, I just wanna show America what it's like to grow up in gangs and at the same time, I wanna show the youth that there are other alternatives besides gang-banging."

"Me and Sabrina wanna be in it," Sabrina stated.

"Alright put your clothes on. The sooner you guys get dressed, the sooner we can start filming," Solomon ordered.

"How are you going to film us? You don't have a camera," Deena asked and answered in the same sentence.

"It's in my car. On Piru I'm not playing," Solomon stated. "Meet me on a hundred and thirty-second street in front of Nine's house."

"Alright," Deena responded. The twins dashed across the street into the house to get dressed, once he swore on his gang affiliation.

"Are you sure, you don't wanna be in the documentary?"

"Yeah, go get the video camera. I have something very special I would like to state to the world," Chinadoll stated. Solomon did not take his mother serious. He knows firsthand that she can be a smart ass from time to time, so he didn't move. Chinadoll became serious. "I'm berious (serious) blood on Piru!"

Solomon ran from his mother's yard, to grab the video camera thrilled that she agreed to be in the documentary. But pondered on what type of statement she's about to make. It doesn't matter, he's just excited that they're doing something together as a family. Chinadoll steps into the house for a moment, only to return with a lit Newport, hanging from in between her lips. Solomon speed walks from his vehicle, back into the yard adjusting the camera, preparing to record. "Alright when I say when, state your name and gang affiliation. Then after that, you can say whatever you feel," Solomon instructed, looking through the lens of the camera making sure the lighting is correct. "Alright, When".

Chinadoll tilted her head slightly closing her right eye, as she took a drag from her cigarette, collecting her thoughts. Seconds later, she blew smoke rings from her mouth before she spoke. "I'm O.G. Chinadoll from West Side Piru Rolling One Thirties and it's C.K. (Crip Killer) all day even on a holiday on mine blood. And for those who don't like it fuck you!

Straight up! Fuck the police, specifically the Carson Sheriff and the Bompton (Compton) dum-dums (Compton police) fuck y'all bitches!

Them suckers dropped my husband O.G. Chinadog off in crab hood and got him killed. I also lost my son to gang violence too. So, if you wanna join this life style do so at your own risk. Because don't nothing come from this shit but death and prison." Chinadoll stated in a serious tone ending her conversation by flashing a gang sign at the camera, in the shape of a "P." Deena and Sabrina came from across the street walking back towards their mother's home dressed in all red tight fitting clothes, exposing their hour glass figures. "Was'sup, blood what that Piru like?" They both shouted in unison waving red bandanas and flashing gang signs with their hands. As Solomon turns the camera towards his twin sisters to get some action; Smurf, Kay-Kay and Vanity turned onto the block pounding 'Dance Floor' by Zapp and Roger Troutman. Deena started doing a dance what is known as the blood walk, on time with the beat. The blood walk is a dance, that is done with a person spelling out the word blood with their feet, onto the ground. Sabrina joined in as the jeep pulled alongside the curb, music still pounding. The females inside the jeep saw Solomon with the video camera and jumped out joining the twins, by blood walking in the middle of the street while flashing gang signs also. Solomon got five minutes of raw and uncut dance footage, before the Pirus became winded. Smurf reached into the jeep and turned the stereo down.

One by one, each female introduced themselves by stating their gang moniker and the denomination of Pirus they're affiliated with. Solomon was excited with the footage he accumulated so far. He walked through his neighborhood, documenting certain areas where Piru members were slained and showing areas where rival Crips were murdered. He recorded alleyways and abandoned houses, that are covered in graffiti, explaining what the scribe meant. Afterwards, he along with his twin sisters and other female Piru comrades, walked around the corner to a 132nd street, in front of Nine's home. There were over ten Pirus hanging out, selling weed and cocaine to anyone who had money. Nine is posted up in the driveway dressed in an all-black khaki suit, with red Chuck Taylors and a black godfather hat, with the red feather on the side, in an all red wheelchair, with a nine-millimeter sticking out of his right front pocket.

Solomon walks into the driveway from the sidewalk, with a huge smile on his face. This is the first time they're seeing each other since he's been home.

"Solo what's up Piru?" Nine asked, throwing up both hands into the air happy to see his young homie.

"Ain't shit blood, what's popping?" Solomon shot back, placing the video camera on the grass giving Nine a long hug.

Soon after, he and all the females that were with him, exchanged hugs and handshakes with the Pirus that were already in attendance.

"What you got there homie?" Nine asked, referring to the video camera while adjusting his hat that Solomon messed up when giving him a hug.

"This is my video camera blood. I'm shooting a documentary about the life style of a Piru gang member. Solomon replied, picking his video camera up off the ground. "Blood do y'all wanna be in it?"

"Hell yeah, I ain't tripping. Anything to support my homies project blood," Nine validated.

Solomon looked to the other Piru members in the yard. "Blood, do y'all wanna be in the documentary?"

"Yeah homie, I ain't tripping," Dirt responded.

"You know I'm trying to get my fifteen minutes of fame, blood," Klown responded joking.

"Just don't record no homies running up to cars, making sales blood, Nine ordered. "Other than that, we all good homie."

"Alright big homie, on Piru you got that," Solomon replied, respecting the big homie's call. "Alright whenever you guys are ready, I'm going to put the camera on each one of y'all. You can say whatever you want."

"What's the purpose of the documentary homie? Are you trying to show the world what we do on an everyday basis? Or are you trying to prevent the youth or anyone else from joining a gang?" Nine asked out of concern.

"Yeah all of that. But, I just wanna show the world the pros and cons of being in a gang," Solomon explained.

"Oh, so you wanna show that Piru love, huh? You wanna show America, that if you're not getting that love in the household, you can get it from your second family a gang," Nine stated, smiling.

"On Piru, you already know where I'm coming from homie," Solomon shot back.

Solomon put the camera on each individual that was in the yard, excluding the females. Each Piru gave their testimony, of how they became involved into gangs. Every Piru that spoke, was articulate and straight to the point. An hour and a half later, Solomon thank'd all of his homies for supporting him, then jumped into the vehicle and went to other Piru neighborhoods in the vicinity: Cedar block, 134th street, 135th street, 142nd street, 151st street, Village Town, Bompton Neighborhood, Fruit Town, Tree Top, Elm Street, Luders Park, Campanella Park, Lime Hood, Holly hood, The Mob, Cross Atlantic, Centerview and Cabbage Patch. Later on that night, he went to Skateland U.S.A. and filmed more Pirus, throughout the greater Los Angeles County. Two weeks has gone by, and Solomon has recorded, a numerous amount of interviews, fights, gang initiations, cars, clothes and anything else that has to do with gang culture. Throughout this whole mission, Solomon noticed that someone was absent; Tina-ru. Solomon asked his sisters and homies of her whereabouts, but each time drew a blank. The only person who saw her lately, was none other than Chinadoll. However, Solomon and Chinadoll had no speaking relationship, so he remains in the dark.

NINETEEN

"Oh yeah, I love your hot cunt baby!" Officer Milano moaned as he grinded, humped and thrusted his five- inch pecker in and out of Tina-ru's pussy at a rapid pace.

Tina-ru is lying on her back on a queen size bed, with her legs spread wide open talking dirty and moaning like she's really into it, as Officer Milano works up a sweat, trying to get a nut." Fuck me daddy, I've been a bad girl. I want all of your huge cock inside of me. Fuck me faster." The dirty talking Tina-ru uttered in a little girl's voice, made Officer Milano hump faster. "Shoot your load all over my boobs daddy."

Officer Milano couldn't take it any longer. He felt a tingling sensation coming from his pinky toe, working its way through his legs and ass cheeks. "Oh, I'm about to cum. I'm about to cum baby."

"Shoot it on me daddy. Shoot it! Come on, quit fucking around!" Tina-ru demanded aggressively, sounding like a desperate white chick.

"Oh shit!" Officer Milano shouted, as he pulled out, shooting cum all over Tina-ru's chest and stomach. "Oh yeah, baby! Yeah, fuck yeah!"

Tina-ru rubbed his eggs all over her chest and stomach, then pulled him by his dick, towards her face, shoving it into her mouth, sucking the remainder of cum that was inside of him. "Mmmm I love the way Italian cock taste in my mouth," Tina-ru lied, pulling Officer Milano towards her, kissing him on the lips. This secret relationship has been going on, the day after Solomon

212

went to Los Padrinos for the handgun last year. Tina-ru was pulled over one night by Officer Milano; soon after going on a hunch, he searched her car and discovered a handgun. Fear of going back to jail, Tina-ru offered false information concerning his wife, Christina Milano and her favorite student Solomon. She painted a picture in his mind, that the two were in a sexual relationship before it happened. This confirmed Christina's attitude and body language towards her husband.

Officer Milano only had one thing in mind, revenge! He's aware that Solomon is the stepson of Chinadog, and has plans of capturing him and dropping him off deep in Compton Crip territory, to get killed or better yet, do it himself. Officer Milano jumped into the shower cleaning himself thoroughly. He returned by the bed dripping wet, drying himself off with a dry towel. "Have you heard anything about Solomon, returning home from jail?"

"No, but it's about that time. I'll swing through the hood later on, and see what I can come up with," Tina-ru explained, slowly climbing out of the bed, cleaning herself off in the bathroom, with a hot soapy face towel. "What if I can get both of them together? Would you like for me to notify you?"

Officer Milano grew a devilish smirk on his face. *Oh, hell yeah! Not if, but when you catch them together, not only am I gonna take the two of them out, but your black ass is going with them! Then I can collect the insurance on my wife!* "Most definitely sweetheart, that's a no brainer." Officer Milano responded, getting dressed. "Don't forget, there's something in it for you too."

Yeah right bitch! You must don't think I know about your crab sympathizing ass getting the big homie killed! Don't trip blood. I'm going to even the score by taking it out on your wife for stealing my man.

"Alright baby, I got you" Tina-ru responded.

"Hey Tina, I have to run baby, keep me updated," Officer Milano, demanded. A naked Tina-ru walked from the bathroom, back into the bedroom by the door, where Officer Milano is standing. "So I guess that means until the next time we meet huh?"

"Yes, I'm afraid so," responded the horny officer, who glances at Tina's curvy figure, growing another erection. He palmed Tina's right breast and swirled his tongue around her crusty black nipple for several revolutions before letting go. "Alright Tina, I'll catch you later." Tina-ru reached towards his face, kissing him on the lips. "Alright baby, keep your eyes open."

Officer Milano exited from the secluded motel room, jumped into a gray Crown Victoria and drove off into traffic. Trailing behind him from a distance, is an identical Crown Victoria same year and color.

September 12, 1988   Sunday 3:45 p.m.

TWENTY

Solomon and Christina are sitting on the couch in his apartment, cuddled up, looking at the final cut of the documentary that he recorded. This Friday, Terry is going to present his film at the Sundance film festival, in West Hollywood, in hopes of being picked up by a major film company. Ninety minutes later, the film left an impression on Christina.

"That was very informative honey. Now I have a clear understanding of gangs and why people join them. I'm willing to bet that a major company is going to pick up that film and broadcast it on television to a broader audience," said Christina, gazing into Solomon's eyes. Christina can no longer hide it. She's deeply in love.

"Man, I hope so. I hope it airs on 48 Hours or Dateline, so the world can be educated about gangs," Solomon responded, pecking her on the lips. "We have to talk it into existence."

"Do you think that method works? Have you ever talked anything into existence?"

"Does it work?!" Solomon chuckled, pulling Christina in closer, kissing her on the lips again. "I talked us into existence, ever since that day, I stood before the class, when you was staring at me with love in your eyes."

"No I was not!" Christina shot back giggling. She began blushing, from Solomon putting her on blast. "No, your little friend Ms. Lucas, was looking at me with malice in her eyes. She couldn't stand for us to be alone in the classroom after school. That's why I used to put her out." *My next move is to put her out*

215

of her misery! I will protect you by any means necessary baby. You are way too intelligent to be associating with a low life like her.

"I know, she didn't like it one bit. But hey, that's life. It's not about her, it's about me and I'm more than happy thanks to you," Solomon expressed, as he unbuttons her shirt and blue jeans.

"I'll do any and everything in my power, to make sure that you succeed Solomon in anything you do. I sympathize with you one hundred percent. I'm a woman that's in love with a Piru, so we must show each other some Piru love," said Christina, stating her thoughts. She began breathing heavily, as Solomon snatched away the last piece of clothing: her panties.

"Well, if you sympathize with me, and have my back one hundred percent, I might as well initiate you in," Solomon expressed, as he quickly removed all of his clothing. He aggressively pulled Christina to the edge of the couch by her legs. Then grabbed her from behind both of her knees, pressing them against her chest, exposing her smooth shaved pussy and asshole. Solomon dropped down onto his knees, and began lapping her asshole, like a thirsty dog, quenching his thirst. Her moans answered every tongue lashing he put on her. After satisfying her anal opening, he munched on her clit like it was his favorite food. Christina moaned, cried and begged him to stop cause it felt so good. Solomon came up for air. "So what are you gonna do?"

Christina deeply loved Solomon and was ready to give all of herself to him. Equally important, she was ready to divorce her husband because the love wasn't there anymore. In addition she was up on his little secret. But now is not the time to bring it to the light. Christina's mind is racing with various thoughts, searching for the right answer. She thought back to the documentary, seeing the two ways that women are initiated into gangs, One, by putting in work against rival Crips. Two, getting sexed in by one of the men. Christina was not about to commit any acts of violence against any rivals, at least as for now. So she decided to get sexed in.

"Solomon, promise me that you're going to be with me forever." she asked, looking into his eyes.

"I promise," Solomon answered, looking into her eyes sincerely. "But what about your husband?"

She grabbed him by both arms, pulling him into to her. "Don't worry about him. I'm ready baby."

Solomon formed a smile on his face kissing her on the lips. He knew that she loved his crusty nuts, but for her to go this far was mind boggling. Solomon flipped her petite frame onto her knees and started hitting her doggy style, while pulling her by her hair. "Do you like it like this, baby?" he asked, speeding up the pace long stroking her. The sounds of sweaty skin and nuts slapping against her pussy, along with her cries of passion echos throughout his apartment.

"I love it daddy, fuck the shit out of me!" Christina cried.

The two had rough sex for an hour in every position. Then they slowed down and started making passionate love, for another hour. After Solomon came inside of her several times they cuddled.

"Do you remember the conversation we had in the classroom that day?" Solomon asked.

"Which conversation baby? You know we talked several times in the classroom honey," Christina responded, placing her head on his chest gently rubbing his nipple.

"When you asked me, where do I see myself in the next five years? Oh yeah, I remember. Why hun?"

"In the next five years, I see us happily married, with children and financially secured," Solomon hinted.

Christina chuckled. "That sounds wonderful honey, but that wasn't your answer. You said at that time, that you're just going through life's adversities. You said that one day, you believe that your experiences, are going to motivate someone to be the best that they can be. Plus, you said that you're gonna be successful, and that you have to talk it into existence," Christina reminded him. "Then you asked me that same question and I told you that my life is going to change drastically, but I'm going to enjoy the change. Everything we spoke on, is unfolding as we speak."

Solomon nodded his head in agreement." That's the power of spoken word."

Christina kissed Solomon on the lips. "Well, honey, I have to go handle some business." She explained, as she stood up getting dressed.

"So, am I going to see you before Friday?" Solomon asked.

"Yes honey, you'll see me before then. I know that you're getting tired of me just up and leaving. Just let a few things work out on its own and we'll be living together in no time baby," Christina expressed, trying her best to comfort. Solomon formed a look of disappointment on his face. She pecked him on the lips one last time before exiting the apartment.

Solomon sat on the couch in deep thought, thinking about the good ol' days he had in Camp 15 with Ms. Crutchfield. It's been ninety days since his release and he has not contacted her one time, after promising to do so. Little did he know, he has made a silent enemy.

*****

The body language between Christina and her husband is obvious, there is no longer a connection. Christina lies in the bed watching the ten o'clock news catching up on current events, thinking about the whooping Solomon put on her pussy earlier.

Her husband walks out of the shower into the bedroom drying himself off, looking at his wife growing an erection. Christina pays him no mind. "Honey, how come we don't make love like we use to huh?"

"I haven't been in the mood lately, baby," she responded, looking at the television, still paying him no mind.

Her husband crawled onto the bed slowly, like a panther, growling. He reached her face and kissed her in the mouth. She kissed him back, but the feeling wasn't there. He felt it and exited the room. She refused to stop him. Ten minutes later, he returned with a red bandana wrapped around his head aunt jemima style and a matching t-shirt, with nothing else on. He stood by the door flashing Piru gang signs with both hands. "What's up blood? Maybe this will get you aroused." her husband stated, dropping an indirect hint being sarcastic.

Christina looked over in his direction, disgusted at what she saw. "What are you insinuating?"

"It seems like you're not turned on by the cops. So I'm going to role play as a Piru," Officer Milano stated, slowly strolling into the bedroom with his fist inside his palm, frowning at his wife, mimicking the characteristics of a gang banger.

Christina removed herself from the bed and got dressed. "I had enough of your shit Donovan. That was the last straw."

Her husband became angry, when he saw her getting dressed. "Where do you think you're going, Christina? Answer me!"

A fully dressed Christina removed her wedding ring from her finger, tossing it onto the dresser. "We are officially separated. I no longer love you Donovan. I hope you have a prosperous life."

"You can't just up and leave like that! I haven't done anything!" her husband shouted, in disbelief that she's really leaving.

"I'm no longer turned on by a cop. I'm turned on by a Piru," Christina declared, grabbing her purse and keys, exiting out the door.

Officer Milano grew numb from her declaration and stood in disbelief, as he watched his ex-wife walk out of their home. Being that he's a Crip sympathizer, he took her statement as a slap in the face. *That little punk turned my wife out. I'm going to do him just like I did his stepfather! Then we'll see how much she's turned on by a Piru!*

December 15, 1988   Thursday 12:15 p.m.

TWENTY ONE

The premier of Terry's documentary was a hit. Two weeks later, it was picked up by the show 48 hours, who broadcast it the following week, instantly making Solomon a household name overnight. Ted Koppel from the Dateline network, offered Solomon a job to speak at various: high schools, group homes, foster homes, and juvenile correctional facilities, in several states, making $1,500 each appearance. Solomon accepted Ted's offer and went on a sixty day tour, that started October 10th, and ended December 10th. Each facility Solomon visited, he met new people in higher places. During his visit at Taft High School in San Fernando Valley, he met a guy by the name of Barry Burris.

Barry Burris is a retired film maker, with numerous hit movies under his belt, who now teaches film making at the University of Southern California. Impressed with Solomon's skills; he offered to teach him the art of film making free of charge. Solomon accepted and enrolled into the class.

Soon after, Christina stopped teaching at Centennial High School. She sold several properties and purchased a McDonald's franchise. Following that, Christina and Solomon moved into a spacious 7,000sq ft. home in Baldwin Hills. With well over $90,000 in his account, Christina showed Solomon how to invest his money into real estate, in which he purchased two tax credit houses, fixed them up and rented them out as rental properties. Solomon talked his success into existence. However, the best is yet to come.

Just like any poor person who gets a taste of the good life, only to return to the neighborhood to throw it into the faces of the less fortunate. Solomon pulls his brand new 1989, all red convertible Corvette, alongside the curb in front of his mother's home.

Being that it's December, today is a gloomy overcast looking day. Solomon climbed out of his Vette, dressed in an all-black Levi matching jeans and jacket outfit and a pair of red suede Wallabees. As he walk towards his mother's front yard, Chinadoll bursted through the front door of her home, dressed in all red clothing excited. She dashed through the front yard, like she won the showcase prize on the price is right.

"My baby!" Chinadoll screamed excitedly, jumping onto her son bear hugging him as if she hasn't seen him in years. Solomon was shocked, but at the same time joyful inside that his mother is finally showing him some affection, that is long overdue. "Baby, I'm so glad to see you. How you been doing, blood?" Chinadoll asked, stepping back, taking a good look at her famous son.

"Shit I'm straight blood. Just been handling my business, trying to make it that's all," Solomon responded, with a huge smile on his face.

Chinadoll looked over at his red Corvette out of admiration, flashing Piru signs with both hands. "That's what I'm talking about blood. You're repping that P-Funk (PIRU) to the fullest. I'm proud of you and love you blood on Piru."

The wells of Solomon's eyes became watery, out of joy from his mother's statement. This is the attention that he's been waiting for from his mother since he was a child. He formed a smile on his face soon after, flashing Piru sign's with both hands at his mother. "That's all I ever wanted from you blood, was for you to tell me that you loved me. Now I feel like a real Piru."

Chinadoll walked up to her son and gave him a long hug. "Forgive me baby I was out of line."

"I forgive you momma," Solomon responded, squeezing his mother back.

"Whuuuut! Say it ain't so!" Deena hollered, from across the street. She and Sabrina walked over to their mother and brother joining them in a group hug. The twins began crying out of joy. "This is how it's suppose to be, blood."

"For real blood on Piru," added Sabrina, stepping back from the group drying her eyes. "Man, I knew this day was gonna come when we could just hug each other and be one big happily family."

"Yeah blood, I apologize to all of you guys for being immature. I was the one holding us back as a family." Chinadoll confessed, taking a cigarette from her pants pocket, placing it in-between her lips lighting it. She took one long drag from the cancer stick and playfully blew the smoke into her children's faces.

Solomon chuckled, fanning the smoke from in front of his face. "Don't worry about it momma we forgive you. We look up to you, you're a Gee (gangster).

"Ain't nobody tripping, we already know you're burnt blood," Deena joked.

They all burst into laughter.

"Blood, you've been getting your feet wet a little bit huh?" Sabrina asked, leaning up against her mother's fence.

"Yeah, I've been doing a little something. Since the documentary was aired on national television, I've been getting job offers left and right," Solomon explained.

"Is that how you got that Vette, blood?" Deena asked.

"Something like that, it was more of a gift from Christina," Solomon responded smiling.

"Who in the hell is Christina? That school teacher?" Deena inquired with attitude, placing her hands on her hips rolling her neck.

Solomon nodded his head. "Yeah, that's my girl."

"Well, we're proud of you I know that much," Sabrina intervened, shifting the conversation.

"Blood, what y'all want for dinner? I'm cooking," asked China, thumping the remainder of the cigarette into the street.

"Say it ain't so. You're about to cook us something to eat?" Deena asked, out of disbelief. She couldn't believe the about face attitude her mother is showing. *I can't believe how mature she's acting! What's up with this trick?*

"Yeah, I'm going to cook my children a meal. What do y'all want to eat?" China repeated.

"Surprise us," said Solomon. "Anything you make is going to be good."

Chinadoll blushed, nodding her head in agreement.

"Alright blood, I got y'all."

Their conversation was interrupted by the pounding bass of rap music, coming from an all-black, 1987 Super Sport Monte Carlo, with black tinted windows, on all gold 15x8, Dayton wire rims. The vehicle pulled in front of Solomon's Corvette. All four Pirus looked at the Monte Carlo, as it parked to see who's going to exit from it.

Tina-ru climbed out the vehicle in all red clothing excited, throwing her hands into the air as she walked up on her homies.

"What's up blood? What that Piru like?" It's been a while since the twins has seen Tina-ru and a first for Solomon since he's been out of jail.

Deena walked up on Tina-ru giving her a hug. "What's up Tina-ru?" "Ain't shit, just bicking (kicking) it," responded Tina-ru.

"What's up homie?" Sabrina asked, exchanging hugs with Tina-ru.

"Ain't nothing, just trying to stay focused," Tina-ru shot back.

Tina-ru looked over at Chinadoll and greeted her, by nodding her head.

China responded by winking her eye and nodding her head in return. Tina-ru was saving the best for last. Once her and Solo made eye contact, she stepped back looking at him from head to toe. She liked what she saw. "What's up superstar? It's about time that I see you in person and not on T.V."

"Hey, what's up Tina-ru?" Solomon asked, giving her a hug, then pulling back.

"Long time no see. The last time I seen you, you were burning rubber down the block pissed off."

"Yeah, that's because you pissed me off blood. You know what you did, but I'm not going there," Tina-ru explained, with a smirk on her face.

While everyone was engaging in small talk, Chinadoll noticed that gray Crown Victoria, that occasionally cruises the hood, unexpectedly. She kept her eye on the vehicle, until it reached the corner, making a right turn onto Avalon Boulevard.

"Blood, what is y'all about to do?" China inquired. I don't like that Crown Vic that just rolled by."

Tina-ru was talking so much, that she didn't realize Officer Milano had passed by her. Oh, shit! She looked down the block, but the car was gone. I'm about to bounce blood, what's popping later on?"

"All of us are going to eat dinner later on, around five o'clock," China responded.

"Where?" Tina-ru inquired.

"At my house, I'm cooking," China replied, as she walked into her yard, headed towards the front door.

Perfect! Tina-ru thought to herself. "Alright, I'll be back by four-thirty. I have to go, I'm riding dirty." "Alright, blood," the twins replied in unison.

"Alright, y'all," Tina-ru shot back. "Alright, Solo, blood."

"Alright, homie," Solomon answered.

Tina-ru jumped in her vehicle and sped off, while the twins went into the house to get dress.

Solomon looked at his mother's kitchen window, hearing sounds of dishes clashing against each other. "Momma!"

"Was'sup blood?" China answered.

"I'll be back. I'm going on the ace. (131st street) to holler at Nine," Solomon explained.

"Alright blood be safe, keep your eyes open too," China insisted.

"All the time," Solomon replied as he walked off. Solomon made it to a hundred and thirty-first street safely. He hung out with Klown and Dirt talking about the good ol' days. Thirty minutes later, Nine and Vanity pulled up on the block in a 1988, convertible Chrysler LeBaron rental car.

"Solo what it do Piru?" asked Nine from the passenger side window.

"Nine, was'sup big homie?" Solo shot back, walking towards the vehicle, to help Nine get into his wheel chair. Dirt and Klown followed behind, to give Solomon a hand with Nine. As they took the wheel chair from the trunk, they all noticed the gray Crown Victoria cruising down Towne Avenue.

"Blood, is that Crown Vic One Time (police) or some crabs?" Nine asked, as his homies pulled him from the passenger side of the vehicle, placing him into his wheel chair.

"This is my first time seeing it," said Solomon, looking in the direction that the Crown Victoria was driving in.

"The reason why I asked, is because that car has been cruising through here lately. Whoever it is we can't see them, because of the dark tint on all of the windows," Nine made it clear, shoving a marijuana joint in between his lips and lighting it. He hit the weed several times choking, before passing it to Vanity.

Solomon glances at his wrist watch. *Damn time is flying. It's four o'clock! I gotta go, I'm not gonna miss my family get together this is big.* "Hey, y'all I'm about to go to mom's house and bick it (kick it) for a while," said Solomon, exchanging hugs and handshakes with his Piru comrades.

"Tell China I said what's up, blood," Nine stated.

"Alright homie, I will," said Solomon, as he walked off. He strolled north on Towne Avenue, singing to himself. As he reached the corner on a hundred and thirtieth street; he sees the gray Crown Victoria slowly pulling to the stop sign on a hundred and twenty-ninth. Solomon became a little nervous, so he played it off by sitting on the fire hydrant, that's on the corner. He turned his body in the direction facing east, so that he could see the Crown Victoria from his peripheral vision. Solomon's heartbeat sped up, as the gray Crown Vic stood at the stop sign, as if the person inside was watching him. Suddenly, the vehicle made a right turn onto Towne Avenue, driving north, stopping at the stop sign on the corner of Towne Avenue and El Segundo Boulevard. Solomon stood up from the fire hydrant, looking in the direction of the gray vehicle. Moments later, there was a break in the traffic, the Crown Victoria slowly made a right turn, with the possibility of driving down a hundred and twenty-ninth street, again. As Solomon started walking towards his mother's home, another gray Crown Victoria pulled up to the stop sign. This caused him to stop dead in his tracks out of fear. He stood still, watching the vehicle make a right turn onto Towne Avenue speeding, then making another right onto El Segundo Boulevard. Solomon was confused, there was no way possible, that gray Crown Victoria went around the corner that fast. He came to the conclusion, that those were two different Crown Vics, that just passed him by. This caused him to speed walk towards his mother's home. As he reaches the corner of a hundred and twenty-ninth and Towne Avenue, the aroma of fried fish lingers into the air. Solomon finally makes it to her home and walks inside. He nods his head to the song, 'Hanging on Strings', by Loose Ends, that's playing from the stereo. He began singing along with the song, as he sits down onto the couch.

Chinadoll strolls into the living room, and turns the volume down on the stereo. "Was'sup blood? The grub is ready, I'm just waiting on the twins and Tina-ru," she explained, walking back into the kitchen.

"Alright I ain't tripping," said Solomon, removing his Levi jacket and placing it on the arm rest of the couch. Solomon continued singing along with the song, playing from the stereo. Five minutes later, Solomon sees the twins exit their home, walking across the street to their mother's home, dressed identical; in red spandex pants, red tank-top baby t-shirts and matching sandals. As they enter through the gate of their mother's front yard, they notice the gray Crown Victoria racing in their direction. "Was'sup blood? What that Piru like?" Deena shouted, at the gray Crown Vic, as it cruised by. The twins both flashed Piru gang signs at the vehicle, before stepping into their mother's home.

"Blood, who was that in that gray Crown Victoria?" Solomon asked the twins.

"I don't know, but they keep driving through here. That fool tint on his windows is pretty dark. Whoever it is, they came through with a hat on trying to disguise themselves," Sabrina explained.

"Is the dude black?" asked China, standing in between the kitchen and living room.

"Yeah, I looked through the front windshield and saw two black dudes the first time. Then every other time, there was one black dude driving by himself," Deena explained.

"Here comes Tina-ru blood," said Solomon, looking through the window, seeing Tina-ru entering through the front yard gate.

"Come in blood," Deena suggested, opening the screen door, so that Tina-ru can come inside.

"What's popping blood? Are we about to grub or what?" Tina-ru asked, rubbing her stomach. "Blood I'm hungry."

"Where did you come from, blood? I didn't see you park your car," Sabrina asked.

"I got dropped off around the corner," Tina-ru explained. "Let me wash my hands blood."

Deena pointed in the direction of the bathroom. "Over there homie."

"Come grab the food homie," Chinadoll demanded, to no one in particular. Deena and Sabrina walked into the kitchen grabbing the food, placing it on the dining room table. Solomon quickly washed his hands in the kitchen sink, then sat at the dining room table. Tina-ru came from the bathroom and joined Solomon at the table.

"What's up blood?" Tina-ru asked Solomon.

Solomon slowly shook his head in disagreement. "Ain't shit, what's popping with you blood?"

In a matter of three minutes, the table was set. Chinadoll and her two daughters sat at the table, preparing to eat.

"Is somebody going to say grace?" Chinadoll asked, to no one in particular. Everyone looked at each other dumb founded. "I'll say it blood, fuck it. Everybody lock p's," Chinadoll ordered. All the Piru members held each other's hand, interlocking p's, then bowed their heads, closing their eyes. "Dear god, thank-you for this food and the nourishment for our bodies. Thank-you for life, the red bandana and a beautiful family, Amen."

"Amen!" Everyone said in unison, soon after placing the P-sign on their chest over their hearts.

The Pirus wasted no time filling their plates with: fried fish, macaroni and cheese, greens and dinner rolls. For ten minutes, the only thing that can be heard is smacking and moans of pleasure. Afterwards, they enjoyed cheese cake with cherry toppings.

The twins removed the leftover food from the table, storing it away inside the refrigerator in zip-lock bags. Twins and Tina-ru sat on the couch, listening to the stereo while their food digested. After Chinadoll cleaned off the table, she stood outside in front of the door smoking a cigarette.

"So what's up blood? When are we gonna get together? You all famous and shit you act like you're too good to fuck with the homies now," Tina-ru expressed, with her lip curled up, sounding foolish. "I heard you and our teacher is messing around. What's up with that?"

Solomon chuckled nonchalantly. "To answer your first question, I don't think I have enough time to fit you into my schedule. Second, yeah, me and Mrs. Milano is an item. That's what's up with that."

The temperature inside her body went up a few degrees, from his reply. "I knew that was in the makings. Was the pussy good? Did she fuck you better than I did?"

Before Solomon could answer, the twins came into the living room with a bottle of Hennessy, a can of coke and some red plastic cups.

"Tina-ru, are you trying to sip or what?" Deena asked raising the liquor in one hand and a can of coke in the other into the air.

"Yeah, blood, pour me a cup. Your brother is over here tripping, on Piru," responded an upset Tina-ru.

"Here", said Sabrina, walking up to her, handing her a cup. Deena followed up, by pouring liquor and soda into her cup. Tina-ru took a few sips and went into chill mode.

Chinadoll stepped back into the house. "Blood pour me some Hen dog."

"Here, I already poured you some," said Sabrina, handing her a cup.

"Good looking," Chinadoll answered. Soon after, she gulped down the half-filled cup belching; then wiped her mouth, with a frown on her face from the taste. "Ba-loood!" Everyone in the living room burst into laughter, from the look on China's face. Chinadoll gulped down two more cups of the brown liquor, within a ten minute period. Five minutes later, the Hennessy kicked in causing Chinadoll to become a little talkative. Tina-ru and the twins became tipsy also from the alcohol.

Solomon watches from the couch, as the four females blood walk to the song 'I can make you dance' by Zapp. Chinadoll started crying hysterically. Deena grabbed her mother to console her, while Sabrina turned the volume down on the stereo. Solomon walked over to where his mother is standing and hugs her. "Blood, you alright?"

"I miss Chinadog and Kyle blood," China sobbed. "On Piru."

Solomon looked at his sisters confused, not knowing what to say. "We all miss them too momma."

Chinadoll snatched away from her son's grip hoo banging, to no one in particular. "THIS P-FUNK BLOOD! WEST SIDE PIRU! C-KAY ALL DAY EVEN ON A HOLIDAY!" Chinadoll yelled, from the top of her lungs, while flashing gang signs. She staggered from the living room through the front door out into the darkness, stopping in the front yard.

"Damn, the big homie twisted blood, on Piru," Tina-ru expressed, bursting into laughter.

"I told you blood your momma is nuts," Deena stated, walking pass Solomon snickering. Deena went out to the front yard, to help her mother get a hold of herself.

"Fuck that, I'm trying to get twisted like moms," said Sabrina, gulping down the remainder of liquor that was inside of her cup. Afterwards, she went outside to help her sister with their mother.

Solomon shook his head out of disappointment. He glanced at his watch realizing that time has flown. *Man, I gotta figure out a way to slide up out of here! I don't wanna be caught up in this goofy shit all night!* He looked over at Tina-ru, who is gawking at him with lust in her eyes. He throws his hands into the air. "This shit is crazy."

"What's up? What are you about to do?" asked Tina-ru walking up on Solomon.

Solomon shook his head. "Nothing, why was'sup?"

Tina-ru looked over her shoulder, to make sure no one was listening. "I'm trying to get some of that super star dick."

Solomon blushed. He knows damn well messing with Tina-ru, would be going backwards. "Oh yeah, from where?"

Tina-ru smacked her teeth. "From you fool."

Solomon played it off by glancing at his watch again. "I have to roll out, I have a few errands to run."

"Damn, white bitch got you on a leash, huh?"

Solomon blushed. "Nawh, that white bitch got me on track."

The twins bring Chinadoll back into the house and place her on the couch. Chinadoll mumbles a few words, then lies down as if she is trying to go to sleep. Solomon walks over to his mother and kisses her on the forehead.

"Awww, that is so sweet. You know you're a good son," Sabrina pointed out, walking up to Solomon giving him a hug. Seconds later, Deena and Tina-ru joined in the group hug.

Solomon blushed, as he returned the love by squeezing the females real hard before letting go. "Well, I gotta bounce," he explained, as he put on his Levi jacket. "Make sure mom is okay. Don't let her go out of the house in the condition that she is in," Solomon demanded, walking to the front door.

"When are you going to slide back through?" Deena asked, with a puppy dog look on her face. "Do you think you can hook me and Sabrina up with a job?"

Solomon nodded in agreement. "I have something better than that. If you and your sister come up with a business idea and plan, I'll put the money up." The twins form smiles on their faces.

"What about me, I have an idea to make some money?" asked Tina-ru, walking towards the front door where Solomon is standing.

"I'm quite sure you do," Solomon responded, with a smirk on his face.

Tina-ru responded by smacking her teeth and rolling her eyes at Solomon. "That white bitch got your nose so wide open. You don't hear nothing I'm saying anymore huh?"

Solomon hunched his shoulders with a smile on his face.

"I'm out blood!" Tina-ru shouted walking past Solomon out the front door.

Everyone snickered from Tina-ru's shenanigans.

"What's up with blood?" asked Deena, referring to Tina-ru.

"Man, I have no idea. She's a little out there, I don't have time for all that drama," Solomon replied.

"You must of put that dick on her huh?" Deena inquired, blushing.

Solomon chuckled. "Why would you say that?"

"Shit, look at the way she's acting," Deena expressed. "Trust me, a bitch knows just by watching another bitch actions."

Their conversation is interrupted by the revving engine and pounding rap music blaring from Tina-ru's vehicle, as she zooms past the house east on 129th street.

Solomon shook his head disgusted. "Well, I'mma holler at y'all later blood." "Alright little bro be safe we love you," Deena expressed, giving Solomon a hug.

"Alright blood," said Sabrina, giving Solomon a hug and kiss on the cheek.

"Alright love y'all, said Solomon as he walked out the front door.

Sabrina watched as her brother walked through the front yard and out the gate, walking to his vehicle, before closing the living room door. "Blood, what kind of business plan do you have?" she asked her twin, walking over to the stereo turning up the volume a few notches. The song 'Heart Breaker' by Zapp is on. Sabrina nods her head to the song, as she straightens up the living and dining room.

"We should open up a beauty salon, we both know how to do hair," Deena responded, removing Chinadoll's shoes from her feet. Moments later, she began helping her sister with getting their mother's house in order.

"Well, we're gonna have to start doing our homework. There are a few buildings up for lease on El Segundo and Avalon. That'll be the perfect spot, it's right in the hood," Sabrina explained.

Deena notices the butt of a handgun sticking out from underneath the side of the couch. She picks it up and shows her sister. "Blood peep game."

Sabrina shakes her head smiling. "Damn, China got the Nina Ross (9mm) up under the couch. She's straight slipping blood on Piru."

Their conversation is interrupted by the sound of screeching tires and rapid gunfire. Off instinct, they both duck down and duck walk to the front door terrified.

"Oh my god! I think Solomon is still out there blood!" Deena shrieked, jumping up and running out the house with pistol in her hand. She notices the gray Crown Victoria on the side of Solomon's Corvette, still shooting. The shooting stops and the vehicle speeds off. Deena ran into the middle of the street firing numerous rounds at the gray Crown Victoria, shattering the back windshield. Sabrina ran towards the Corvette screaming. After emptying the clip of her handgun, Deena joined her sister horrified.

"Solomon! Solomon!" Sabrina yelled, from the top of her lungs. She stood from the sidewalk crying hysterically, looking at her brother's bloody body barely moving inside. The Corvette was riddled with bullets and every window was shattered.

"Blood, I'll be back. I gotta get rid of this pistol," Deena explained, as she ran towards her grandmother's home crying hysterically. Moments later she returned opening the passenger's door of the car, to see if her brother is still alive "Solomon! Solomon!"

"Somebody call the ambulance blood!" Sabrina screamed, dropping to her knees on the sidewalk.

Within minutes, the crime scene was filled with neighbors who live on the street and Piru members. Their grandmother came across the street crying hysterically, on the side of her grandson's vehicle. She called Solomon's name several times, getting no response from him. Everyone looked inside at Solomon's lifeless body, chalking him up as dead.

Several Pirus began throwing tantrums, fleeing the scene to retaliate on the Crips in the area. Moments later, the Carson Sheriff arrives to the scene asking questions; no one cooperated with the authorities. Soon after, the ambulance arrived reviving Solomon and taking him to Martin Luther King, Jr. Hospital. An hour after Solomon was shot, four Compton Crips were murdered.

December 16, 1988   Friday 5:35 a.m.

TWENTY TWO

Four unmarked cars quietly pulls in front of Chinadoll's residence. Eight officers exit their vehicles wearing bullet proof vests, huddling up outside of her fence armed with handguns and a hand held battering ram. After a few words were exchanged between the officers, they rushed through her front yard in a single file line.

The first officer began pounding on the door with the bottom of his fist. There was no reply so the cop pounded on the door again. "Open the door this is the police!" demanded the officer. When he got no response, he gave the guy standing next to him the okay to batter ram the door open. On the second ram, the front door flew open. All eight officers inched their way through the living room screaming and yelling with their pistols drawn. Chinadoll, still a little intoxicated is awakened by all the noise.

"What the fuck is y'all doing blood?!" China asked, sitting up on her elbows.

"Don't move! I'll fucking kill you!" one officer screamed, pointing his gun inches from China's face.

"Cuff her ass up!" demanded another officer in the background.

"Cuff me up for what fool?" China asked, preparing to sit up on the couch, even with the pistols still drawn, inches from her face.

239

"I said don't fucking move!" the first officer repeated. The officer in the background slapped the cuffs on Chinadoll. Once she was cuffed, all the officers placed their guns in their holsters.

"What the fuck is wrong with y'all bitches, busting up in my spot like this blood?! This West Side Piru no cut!" China vented, laying onto her side on the couch.

A gray haired pudgy built white man wearing glasses, walked up on China. "Linda Spencer, you are under arrest for the murder of Daryl Bacon and the attempted murder of Maurice Watts," explained the officer. "Search the premises for the murder weapon," he ordered to the other officers.

Aww blood! This crab ass nigga came back to life and told on me?! Fuck! I knew I should of domed his ass instead of shooting him in the back. China thought, shaking her head out of disappointment.

The officers took over an hour searching Chinadoll's house, looking for the murder weapon. After realizing the gun was not in the house, they grabbed China and placed her in the back seat of the police car. China's mother and two daughters watched from their front yard from across the street, disappointed. A small group of neighbors and Pirus looked on from the sidewalk on both sides of a hundred and twenty-ninth street. Twenty minutes later, the officers piled in all the vehicles and sped off. Not before Piru members shouted gang slogans and flashed gang signs at them.

*****

It's been three weeks since Solomon has been in the hospital. After two surgeries, his health improved going from critical to stable. His room stays crowded with visitors, strangers,

240

gang members, fans and police who constantly interrogate him trying to get a description of the shooters. Nevertheless, Solomon remains silent to the authorities' questions being uncooperative.

Today was a long day for Solomon. Christina stayed with him as long as she could, until they kicked her out which was around 8:05 p.m. Solomon instantly fell asleep taking a two hour power nap. There are two other beds in the room with him, however, they're empty. As Solomon lay sleeping lightly, he can feel someone's presence in the room with him.

The presence comes closer, standing beside his bed looking at him. Solomon is too scared to open his eyes, so he continued to play asleep. His heartbeat rate goes up on the monitor on the opposite side of his bed.

The presence began mumbling a few words in a low whispering tone. Solomon unable to hear, couldn't make out what they were saying. Whoever this person was, stopped speaking for a moment to clear their throat, then started speaking again; this time more clearly. The voice began ranting and raving about being a victim and wondered why it happened to them. Once Solomon recognized the voice, he let out a long and loud gasterous fart. He couldn't believe that this person was standing over him. But for what reason? *What the fuck? Is this fool trying to do me or what?* Solomon thought, shaking like a snitch in a gangster party.

"This is your idea of Piru love muthafucka?" the voice growled, through a set of clenched teeth, covering his eyes with their right hand and covering his nose and mouth with a neatly folded red bandana in their left hand.

The more Solomon bucked, the more pressure this anonymous person applied.

"Spencer...Spencer are you okay?" asked a female nurse from a distance, coming towards his room.

The person who attempted to take Solomon's life, let go of his face and dashed towards the door fleeing the scene. As they were exiting the room, the nurse was coming in. The assailant bumped into the nurse hard, almost knocking her down.

"Excuse me, there is no running in the hospital. You could have at least said excuse me," stated the female nurse, as she adjusted her uniform, watching the female assailant get in the wind. "Crazy bitch," the nurse mumbled, as she walked into Solomon's room. A horrified Solomon was sitting up in his bed sweating profusely. The nurse took the folded red bandana from the top of his chest and patted Solomon's head dry with it. "Mr. Spencer, did you know that woman who ran out of here a minute ago?"

Solomon was too scared to speak, he just nodded in agreement. *Out of all the people that I know, she tried to kill me?* He was puzzled as to why she was trying to take him out. He thought they departed on good terms. He just simply laid back into the bed in deep thought, numb from the multiple questions that the nurse was asking.

THE END

ALSO WRITTEN BY KRE-KRE COMING SOON...

PIRU LOVE

Part 2

(Coming soon)

Made in the USA
San Bernardino, CA
27 January 2020